CRIMINALS
a novel

Ben Masaoka

Propeller Contemporary Fiction
Propeller Books
Portland, Oregon

Copyright © 2024 by Ben Masaoka

All rights reserved. Except for brief passages quoted in critical articles or reviews, no part of this book may be reproduced in any form or by any means, electronic or mechanical, including photocopying and recording, or by any information storage and retrieval system, without permission in writing from the publisher.

For further information, email publicity@propellerbooks.com.

First U.S. edition, 2024
Cover and interior design by Dan DeWeese
Cover photo (top) courtesy of the author
"Ballona Creek channel with palm trees silhouetted at sunrise" by Jengod, used under CC BY 4.0 / tinted from color original

10 9 8 7 6 5 4 3 2 1

Published by Propeller Books, Portland, Oregon
ISBN 978-1-955593-10-6

www.propellerbooks.com

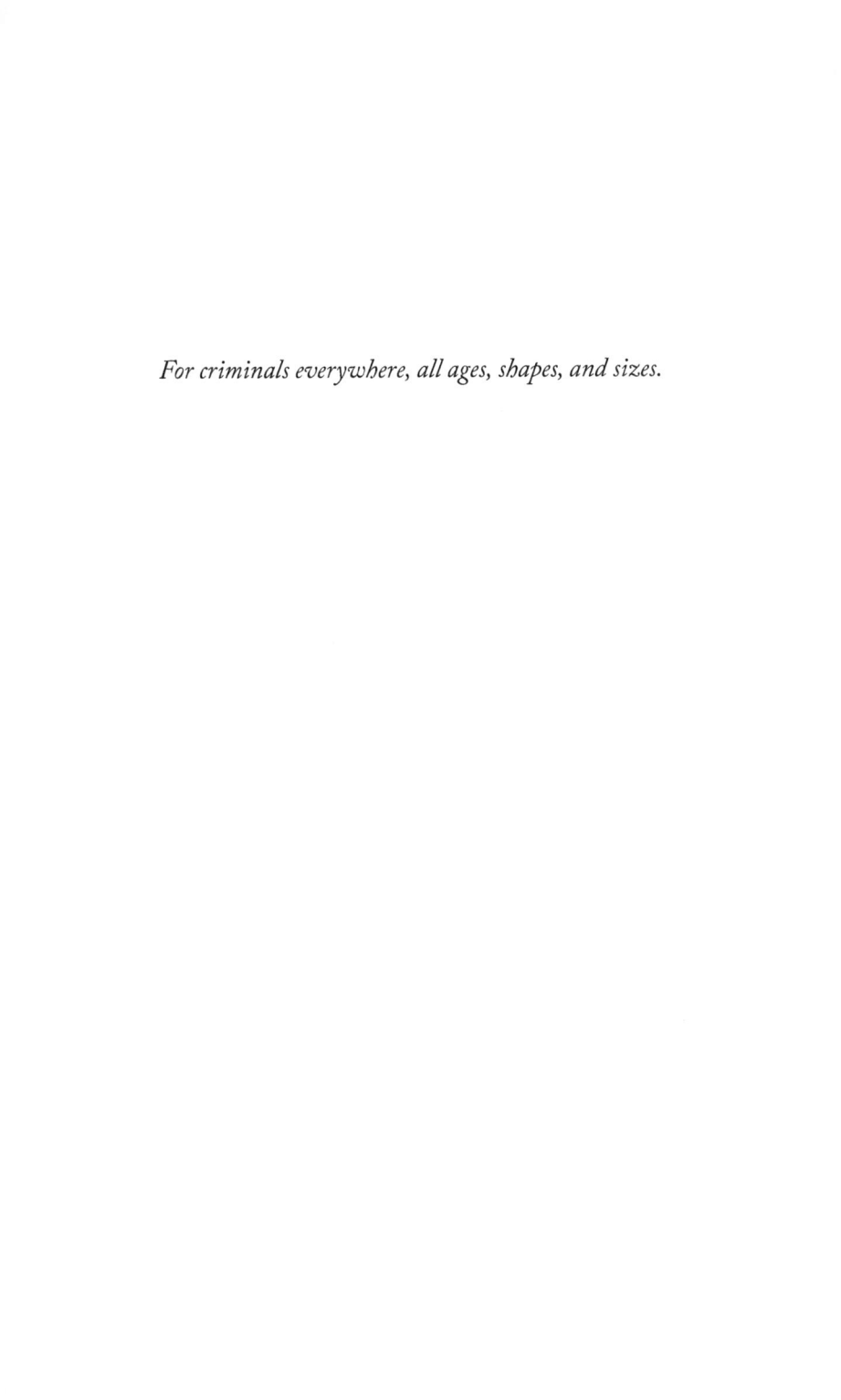

For criminals everywhere, all ages, shapes, and sizes.

CRIMINALS
a novel

Chapter One

THE TANAZAKI house is a quiet house. With cautious steps Hank follows the plastic carpet runner through the living room, careful not to make a sound. He trails his finger across a small wooden table where family photographs are placed. One of the family together, one of Kazu and Alice, a school photo of Ruth in the third grade, a school photo of Hank in kindergarten. Walking past, he draws a trail through dust on the table to see what his mother wants. He is five years old.

On this hot day the thin curtains in her bedroom sway inward when Hank opens the door. A faint medicinal smell pervades the room. As he passes the vanity he glances at the little tools, powders, and lotions his mother hasn't used for a long time.

"Water, please."

She speaks in a whisper. There are times she does not recognize who he is. On some days she peers from the bed. "Hank?" she will ask, her face barely lifting from the pillow, her eyes puffy slits. It frightens Hank when his mother does not know him.

He takes her glass, smudged along the rim from her lips, and runs to the kitchen. Ruth monitors how he fills the glass with water.

"Not so much, she'll spill it."

Ruth is eight years old and considers herself in charge of Hank. Hank pours a little out.

He returns to Alice's room and watches her rise on her elbow to drink, set the glass on a bedside table next to a cowbell, and lower herself back down. He knows she grew up on a farm in Idaho where the cowbell on the table used to hang from the neck of a brown cow named Pudding. He likes to imagine Pudding's tail flicking away flies as he has seen cows do on television. The bell is painted white, it makes a clangy sound. Alice uses it to call for them. She is pale and tired looking. Strands of black hair stick to the side of her face.

Her dark eyes seem half asleep. Then a smile appears, just a little one. She is looking at him. He steps closer until his knees touch the bed. Hank wants to reach out to her, but instead he turns and runs back into the kitchen.

They live at the end of a dirt road alongside Ballona Creek in Los Angeles. It is 1957. Celery fields to the west give way to mudflats, marshes, and in another mile or two the ocean. Their house is a small rambler, painted white. In the summer heat the lawn is turning brown. A rock garden meant to look Japanese—there is a withered pine tree only two feet high—is overgrown with weeds.

Later, Hank hears his father's truck pulling around the house into the backyard, and he turns to see Ruth run outside. He watches her go, picturing how Ruth will help Kazu, their father. Hank used to help as well, knowing where the mowers, watering hoses, clippers, rakes, canvas tarps, shovels, and gasoline cans are kept. Hank knew the smell of his father's clothing, of earth and cut grass, and the dirty, floppy cap smelling of sweat. Then Hank did something wrong. He never knew what. All he remembers is his father's shouting, Ruth's staring, anxious face. Now it's only Ruth who helps unload tools and plants and accompanies Kazu across the patio into the kitchen carrying his thermos and brown scheduling notebook.

Hank is silent when they come inside. He never knows what to say. His father is like a castle with a moat around him full of dangerous things.

Kazu is wiry and tan, with thick black eyebrows. He unlaces his boots and glances at Hank in the kitchen. Hank stays where he is.

"Hank got Mommy water the most times today," Ruth says.

"Good job, buddy boy," Kazu says, pulling off his boots.

Ruth smiles at Hank.

Kazu washes his hands and sets about making dinner. He opens a can of Spam and cuts the pink jellied meat into thin cakes. As they are frying he slices a tomato and looks to see if the rice is done.

Ruth sets plates and glasses on the table, Hank gets silverware.

Alice joins them. She has washed her face and brushed her hair. It's been awhile since she's come out for dinner. Her old blue Muumuu has white flowers. Hank remembers she called them Hawaiian flowers.

There is Ruth across the small table from him, Kazu next to her, and he next to Alice. He and Ruth can make faces at each other while they eat.

Alice turns to him. "Hank, will you say prayers?"

He bows his head. "Dear God, thank you for the food. Please bless Mommy and Daddy, and Ruth and me. Thank you. Amen."

Hank looks up. Kazu and Alice still have their heads bowed. Ruth is staring at him. She moves her mouth to form silent words. *In Jesus's name. Amen.*

"In Jesus's name. Amen," Hank repeats.

He's been told it does not count unless he says that.

"I'm only having rice," Alice says. She cuts her Spam in half for Hank and Ruth to share.

Kazu's face has a pleasant look as he chews his food.

"Today I got another client in Beverly Hills. Now I have four houses there."

Alice murmurs in appreciation. "So nice of Mr. Ito to give you the first house."

"I'll get him a bottle of whisky."

"I wonder if Etsu will like that? How about a nice plant?"
"A plant? He's a gardener. He can get his own plants."
"Yes, Mommy, he can get his own plants!" Hank giggles, then stops, his eyes dart to his father.
"Sam likes whiskey."
"Make saké for him," Ruth says.
"So much talk of alcohol."
"Did Jesus drink wine?" Ruth asks.
"Yes, but only a little."
"Jesus has long hair," Hank says.

Instead of going to bed after dinner, Alice sits in the living room to watch television while Ruth and Hank clean the kitchen. Hank sweeps. He considers himself a good sweeper. With the straw broom he gets everything into a pile. Pieces of food, dirt from his father's boots, hair. He even sweeps up an ant that keeps trying to crawl away. He empties the dustpan into the trash container under the sink. Looking up out the window he sees the sky is already dark.

It is his job to take out the trash. He flicks on the outside light that dimly illuminates a small circle on the dirt driveway. The backyard seems far away, part of a darkness that includes farmland next to the house. In the distance are tiny yellow windows of shacks where Mexican workers live. Except for that small comfort there is only the night, quiet but for the sound of insects swarming the overhead light. Spiders lurch across their webs, feasting.

He lingers at the edge of the light, searching the darkness with his eyes, then takes a deep breath and steps into it.

It always surprises Hank how well he can see in the dark. But that is the problem. He walks past the wood pile and wonders if, at night, it only pretends to be a wood pile. Tall eucalyptus trees, gently swaying beneath the afternoon sun, are now aware and bend towards him with intent. After what seems a long walk he reaches the bamboo fence in front of the garbage cans. Here is the worst part. Anything can hide behind the fence, behind the cans themselves, behind the small shed where his father stores things they never use. Hank gathers himself and steps past the fence into a darker dark, keeping his eyes focused on the metal lid of the garbage can. He lifts it off and places it quietly on the ground. He feels a presence, but Ruth told him never to look. He empties the trash and replaces the lid. He forces himself to turn his back on whatever is creeping up, reaching for him, and walk, not run, to the house. He reenters the circle of light and is safe.

Ruth watches TV with their mother. He sits on the floor next to Alice's legs and leans his head against them. Her bony knees. He likes how she smells. She strokes his hair.

It is Lawrence Welk and the Lennon Sisters. Hank imagines that when he marries it will be either to Ruth or their mother. But he also loves the Lennon Sisters, each of them are beautiful and gracious, more so it seems to him than his own mother and sister. Watching them dance and sing he feels a vague discomfort, as though his admiration is disloyalty to his family.

After the show Alice asks Ruth to turn off the TV and they sit together for a while. From inside the bathroom comes the sound of the shower and the ballgame on the radio. The announcer shouts, his voice rises excitedly in a blur of words. Kazu has a colostomy from the war and twice a week he takes an enema. "Enema Night," they call it. To Hank it means sports games on the radio and a steamy bathroom afterwards that smells like sweet fertilizer.

As if thinking about Kazu and his war injury, Alice says, "God loves those who suffer."

She often makes announcements out of the blue. *The Lawrence Welk Show* is over, why not talk about God?

To Hank, God is his mother propped up in bed reading the Bible, underlining words and writing with a red pen on the sides of the pages. God is the voice of the preacher that comes from the transistor radio every Saturday, which she calls the true Sabbath.

God is his mother kneeling on the floor beside her bed in her nightgown, eyes closed, hands clasped. Hank has seen her like this and has heard his name in her mumblings. God is how his mother sometimes looks at him as from a distance, as though in consideration of something that, he doesn't know why, makes him anxious and afraid.

Alice tucks them into bed when she feels well enough to read from the Bible. Tonight, after the stories from Revelation are over and Alice closes the black, leather-bound book, Hank wants to keep her there. "Can we look at the Noah's Ark pictures?" he asks.

"Yes."

He hops up and goes to a small bookshelf and finds the one he wants. He is fascinated by the grainy drawings of men and women drowning, clawing at the sides of the ark. The gray rain falls upon upturned faces filled with terror and regret. Their bulging eyes stare heavenward.

"Is it too late for them, Mommy?" he wonders.

"Yes."

"I don't see animals in the water," Ruth says.

"All the animals are in the ark," Hank explains, looking from Ruth to Alice.

"No, just two of each," Ruth says. "Shouldn't there be other animals in the water, floating with the humans?"

Alice closes the book.

"Someday," she says, "men will come and tell you to spit on the Bible, or they will cut off your heads."

Her voice is grave. She turns her eyes from Ruth to Hank.

"You must not spit on the Bible. Let them cut off your heads. Do you understand?"

"Yes."

"Yes, Mommy."

Alice studies their faces.

"Or the men will say, 'Spit on the Bible, or we will cut off your Mommy's and Daddy's heads.' But tell them, 'No.' Do not spit on the Bible. Let them cut off Mommy's and Daddy's heads."

Hank whimpers. Ruth's face is pale and expressionless.

"Don't worry, because Mommy and Daddy will see God."

"Yes."

"Yes, Mommy."

"Do you promise? Don't you want us to see God?"

"We promise."

Hank's lips tremble, he clutches the blanket to him.

Alice stares at them.

"The men will tell Mommy and Daddy, 'Spit on the Bible, or we will cut off the heads of your children.'"

Hank and Ruth barely breathe.

"Do you want to be with God?"

Ruth whispers, "Yes."

Hanks moves his lips silently with his sister's, unable to take his eyes away from Alice's face.

Alice reaches out, taking their hands into hers. Her eyes are not sad at all.

"Mommy, when will this be?"

She squeezes their hands.

"Soon," she says.

Hank lies awake in the dark, imagining plagues of rotting skin and seas of blood. He imagines his mother's face as the men threaten her with what will happen if she does not spit on the Bible. The faces of those men, the same faces floating in the water next to Noah's ark, turn to look at him and Ruth.

To Hank, Ruth looks like a tall, skinny boy because of the short haircut Kazu gave her. Their haircuts always look the same, as if their heads were bushes their father had to prune back for the season. As they walk along the dirt road to the mailbox on Centinela Avenue, Hank gazes up at his sister, liking how their hair is the same.

"Too early," Ruth says, peering into the empty box. Hank looks into it after she does.

He likes the dirt road they live on. During the winter rains, cars get stuck and dig long furrows in the mud that dry to become ruts he now walks upon, crushing down the sides, dirt getting between his toes. Along the road is Ballona Creek, its flat water empties into the ocean beyond the far end of the fields. At high tides the ocean pushes into the creek with small rolling swells. They stop to throw rocks, standing on the high bank and shielding their eyes to stare at the water glinting bluish in the noonday sun. At other times the water is green with algae, or even gray with oil streaks. This is Los Angeles, after all. Walking carefully, they can go all the way down the steep concrete slope of the bank to the water and catch tadpoles, but today they wear flimsy rubber slippers that aren't good for it. Standing at the top of the high bank Hank throws a rock as far as he can. The rock bounces down the slope and rolls into the water with a plop. Ruth throws her rock that arcs through the air and splashes a few yards from shore.

They always throw rocks together but Hank can never hit the water.

"Someday you'll throw rocks as far as me," Ruth says, smiling at him. Her short hair, her glasses, her tall awkwardness. He doesn't care if she is pretty or not, only that she is his sister, trustworthy and kind. When Kazu becomes angry and yells at Hank, Ruth sits with Hank afterwards, her arm around his shoulders, and tells him how to behave better so he can stay out of trouble. Or she tells stories to make him forget their father's anger. She told Hank about a being that lives in the large tunnel in the side of the creek, a cave-like opening to the vast underground drainage system beneath the city. As she described the creature living in the subterranean world,

Hank thought he remembered seeing it once or twice, a pair of eyes staring from the darkness of the tunnel.

She takes his hand and they continue along the dusty, rutted road. To the side of their front yard is a large willow tree. Hank loves the tree. Ruth explained that once upon a time a girl sat waiting for so long she turned into the willow. "And her spirit lives in the tree." He thinks of the tree as a girl with long, flowing green hair. During art hour in kindergarten he painted the tree. The teacher told him it's not how real trees look. "Do it over," she said.

The heat makes him lazy. Back in the room he and Ruth share he lies on the cool, dark green floor while Ruth goes to check on Alice. Pressing his cheek against the floor he sees cobwebs under the small desk and tangled electrical cords, the cat's eye marble he thought he lost, orange peels he kicked under the dresser instead of picking up, a comic book under his bed, and a pair of socks under Ruth's bed. The expanse of green floor tiles stretch before him. There is movement in the distance, a beetle crawling, a large stink bug, dragging a string of dust. Hank is a giant lying in this world.

Chapter Two

THAT SUMMER a feral cat appears in their yard. The cat is gray with dark stripes, white paws, and white at the tip of its tail. They see it by the woodpile one afternoon.

"It's hunting lizards," Ruth whispers.

They approach slowly. The cat freezes, stares, then turns and slips away. They see it again in the field, stopping once to turn and look back before darting behind tumbleweeds.

The next day they see the cat lurking around the garbage cans.

"Here, kitty kitty," they squat down and pretend they have food, rubbing their fingers together. But the cat is wild and independent with fierce, narrow eyes.

"Here, kitty kitty," Hank says, moving closer. Again, the cat disappears.

Later that summer, they play in the backyard when Alice is napping. A faint mewing comes from the fields. They find the cat in a little den of bushes, lying in the dirt with kittens crying and suckling. The cat is startled and half rises as if to run away. But the children stay at a distance and talk with soothing voices and it lays back down, watching them warily.

They go to the house and return with a piece of bologna. They toss it to the cat, who tenses, then sniffs it. She quickly stands and eats as the mewing kittens fall to the side.

There is a can of tuna fish in the pantry and they bring that to the hungry cat as well. This time the cat lets them come a little closer.

Ruth knows what their father will say. "I work to feed us, not the cat."

The next day when their mother is napping, she tells Hank, "Follow me."

It is early afternoon. She leads him to the creek where they scoot down the embankment. It is low tide and islands of sand form in the long pools of water. Mud hens float and swim away at the sight of the children, but not far, and continue feeding, dipping themselves upside down among water weeds for worms and bugs in the muck. Ruth has crackers she put in her pocket during lunch and shows them to Hank. He wonders what she is thinking.

She searches along the shore for the right size rock. Ruth is skillful with rocks and likes finding heavy boulders to lift and toss in the water to splash like bombs. She finds a large flat rock and carries it to the water's edge. In bed last night she imagined everything she will do, even the exact order of doing it, summoning the mud hens, lifting the rock and when to throw. "Here muddy muddy," she chants, tossing cracker crumbs in the water at her feet. She has fed them before. The birds paddle over and crowd together, grunting and darting forward. Ruth lifts the rock and holds it over her head. Then she hurls it downward. Two of the birds get away, but not the one in the middle. The bird floats in the water without moving.

Ruth finds a stick and pulls the dead bird to the bank. They examine the dull, dark feathers and black scaly feet. Ruth holds the bird upside down by its skinny legs and climbs the embankment. Hank follows behind, watching the bird's head wag loosely from side to side. In the field they slowly approach the mother cat and her litter. Not coming too close, Ruth gently tosses the dead bird to where the cat lies watching them. It sniffs, then leaps up, scattering the kittens, and pounces on the bird. The cat tears into the breast and growls as it eats. Later that day they return to see a gaping, bloody hole in the body of the mud hen. The mother cat is nursing the kittens and appears less afraid, twisting her head on the ground and gazing up at them.

The next day there are two boys in the field standing several feet apart, playing catch with something. "Get a rock," Ruth says. She runs and Hank follows. The boys are older, junior high age, tossing a kitten to each other and laughing. The mother cat races back and forth looking upward to follow the kitten as it is tossed through the air.

"Stop it! Stop it!"

The boys turn at the sound of Ruth's voice. They stand waiting. The boy holding the kitten drops it to the ground. He raises his foot as if to stomp on the kitten, then lowers his foot and both boys laugh. Ruth flings her rock and hits the boy in the face. His hands fly up as he staggers back and falls. The other boy comes at them. Hank throws his rock, but it sails off to the side. It does not matter. Ruth attacks the boy. He is bigger but she claws him in the eyes before he can grab her. She kicks his shins. Hank does too. They kick and punch him as fast as they can. The other boy climbs to his feet and both run away.

"Will they come back?"

"They better not."

They count the kittens. They are safe.

The next day they return to the field with a piece of fish Ruth knows the mother cat will especially like.

"Can we keep a kitten?" Hank wonders.

"We have to wait until they're older."

"And then?"

"And then we can each have one. They'll keep mice and rats away."

But the bushes and tumbleweeds have been stomped down, the nest wrecked. Among the trampled brush someone has done to the kittens what Ruth did to the mud hen. All are dead, including the mother, crushed by rocks.

At least once a month Dr. Kiyonaga comes to their house to check on Alice.

Ruth watches as he holds her mother's wrist and silently looks at his watch. He wraps a piece of fabric with a dial and a tube around her arm and studies the dial as he squeezes a black ball. He peers into her eyes, ears, nose, and mouth. He gently feels her throat. Ruth's favorite part is when he places the stethoscope's silver disk against her back and chest and listens. Ruth wishes to hear for herself but is afraid to ask.

As he is leaving, Kazu sends Ruth after the doctor with a bag of oranges.

"Dr. Kiyonaga!"

He stands leaning against his car in the late afternoon, smoking a cigarette, jacket draped over his arm. To the west the sun is climbing down the sky.

"My dad says to give you this."

"Oh. Hey, tell him thanks," the doctor says, looking inside.

She does not run back to the house as she normally would. She waits, having a question to ask. But now, alone with him, she's not sure if it's allowed. Adults have so many rules and she doesn't know them all.

"Everything okay, Ruthie?"

She decides it will be okay. "How do I become a doctor?"

"A doctor? Hmm." Dr. Kiyonaga looks at her with a smile. He is a pleasant man with thin hair, a clean-shaven face, and bright, kind eyes. "Well, you have to study a lot, and work hard, and be dedicated. And then you will succeed."

"Will I really?"

"Yes. Of course!"

That night Ruth cannot sleep. She imagines having her own bag of medicines and instruments, a stethoscope to wear around her neck. She thinks about what Dr. Kiyonaga said over and over in her mind. "You will succeed," he told her.

The next day Ruth tells Hank, "When I grow up, I'll be a doctor."

Hank does not know what to say. He opens his mouth and stares.

At dinner Hank says, "Ruthie is going to be a doctor."

It's just the three of them. Alice is in her room.

"Can she be a doctor?"

"Maybe a nurse. That's a good job." Kazu seems pleased with the idea. "It's not bad if the wife works after the children grow."

Ruth sees Hank look at her with a grin. But she turns her eyes down, examining the food on her plate.

In their room that night she ignores Hank's attempts at conversation. He asks questions from his bed in the dark, trying to make her say something, but she remains silent. Soon he is snoring. She thinks about what her father said at dinner. It seems she can't be a doctor, but maybe a nurse.

The next morning, Ruth wakes Hank when she hears Kazu leave for work. They go outside to the row of iris plants in the front yard. She directs Hank to part the slender plants at the soil. Droplets of dew roll down the long, green-smelling leaves. They gather snails into an empty Campbell's soup can. Last night she thought it all out and decided she will begin her doctor training in secret. She feels guilty, a small act of betrayal to her father.

Later that day Ruth makes lunch for Alice, waits for her mother to eat, then retrieves her dishes to wash and put away. She dutifully waits longer to see if Alice needs help walking to the bathroom, and she does. Ruth pauses inside the bathroom door, as always, to let Alice step forward and turn around before steadying her mother as she sits on the toilet. Ruth withdraws and shuts the door. In the living room where she can still hear the toilet flush she waits, arms crossed. Finally she returns Alice to bed, glad it is done for now, knowing she will do it again later. The tasks are always the same. The toilet, fixing meals that Alice never eats. A waste of Ruth's efforts and the uneaten food. She used to feel proud to help her mother, to see the look on Kazu's face when she did, but now it's just a chore she tries to finish as quickly as she can.

"Hank!" she calls, marching into the backyard. Hank appears with the coffee can and she tells him to gather twigs. Hank shows her what he finds.

"Too big," she says.

"Too small," she says.

"Too flimsy," she says.

They finally have several that pass her inspection. On the short driveway at the garage door she shows Hank how to rub the twigs on cement and sharpen the twigs into scalpels.

"Like this."

Hank does as she instructs. She examines his work and says it will do.

Ruth finds a wooden plank from the woodpile to use as an operating table.

"Wait," Ruth says, and runs back to the house. She tears sheets from a pad of blank paper and staples them together into a thin pamphlet. She digs through junk in the kitchen drawer to find a ballpoint pen. She rejoins Hank, who sits on the ground with the tin can, watching snails crawl up the sides. He uses his finger to push and make them fall back down. Ruth shows him the pamphlet she made.

"Mommy writes in her Bible. I'm going to write in this." It is the one thing her mother does that Ruth admires.

"Okay," Hank yawns.

She lays out their twig scalpels.

"See how this one is very straight?"

"Yes."
"It is to be used first."
"Okay."
"See how this one is curved?"
"Yes."
"It is for special uses."
"Okay."

Patiently working, with great delicacy, Ruth removes the shell from a snail. It does not seem affected by the loss. Its eyestalks reappear and it crawls away.

"Now it's a slug."

She writes in her pamphlet, *snail slug*.

It takes a couple of days and many snails, but when she is finally able, using a technique she develops with a bent twig, to remove the entire shell cleanly in half, Ruth is satisfied with her skill. During that time Hank observes carefully. Then he tries it himself. Ruth guides him.

"Be careful. You see how the shell is breaking?"
"Yes."
"Now look what you've done."
"Sorry."
"Be dedicated and you'll succeed."

"Okay," he says, and tries again, grinning as she encourages him. When he does it right she says, "Perfect, Hank!"

He looks at her with his large eyes. Ruth always thinks of everything before he does. He enjoys waiting for her to think of what they can do, and then he follows.

Not far from their house is a dirt lot with a few old wooden buildings. One building is the Japanese language school, one is an all-purpose room for ikebana classes and other crafts, and one is a bare room with a canvas mat on the floor to practice judo. Judo classes for young children are on Saturdays and Ruth wants to learn, but Kazu works on Saturdays and she has to stay home to care for Alice.

Kazu encourages Hank to go. "It's the best thing for a boy!" he says. Hank sees his father's eyes are lively, as if the thought of Hank practicing judo excites him.

"I want to box, like you did."

"Sure, sure. Box later. Add judo to boxing. No one can beat you!" Kazu smacks Hank on the shoulder and smiles at him.

"Okay!" Hank says, glad at what he sees in his father's face. Hank charges away with his fists balled, punching the air.

Each Saturday Hank walks by himself across the fields and two blocks further carrying a rolled-up gi slung over his shoulder. At the dojo he suits up and stands with other boys. Hank does not understand what the judo teacher wants. The teacher points and performs a movement, then stares at Hank silently. It is a puzzle Hank must solve without an explanation. The only clues he receives are smacks on the head from Sensei Yamamoto.

"*Baka!*"

Hank wants to understand why he is being called an idiot, one of the few Japanese words he knows. It must be something he did with his judo partner, or failed to do, that attracted Sensei's attention.

It could be a number of things: his grip on uke is too loose or too tight; the steps he takes are too wide or too narrow; his entry into the throw is too hard or too soft. Or ten other mistakes he must figure out on his own. It seems he can do nothing right. As the summer passes he improves only his ukemi, the art of falling down.

When Hank returns home each Saturday from judo, Ruth takes him to the front lawn and demands to learn everything he learned, even though Hank has just been there and is tired.

"Okay," he grumbles, putting his gi jacket back on and tying his white belt.

He teaches her ukemi, how to grab the opponent, what to do if someone tries to choke or punch, how to trip or throw the opponent to the ground. Ruth practices every day, making Hank grab and push her over and over until she sees how the countermovements work.

"If I push, you pull. If I pull, you push," Hanks says, repeating what Sensei Yamamoto shouts at him, but leaving out the slap on the back of his head. Although he attends classes and Ruth does not, she soon becomes more skillful, and frightens him with her violent energy.

Judo is hard! At the dojo the other boys slam him to the mat, pin him with armlocks until his elbow begins to break, and choke him into unconsciousness. Later, at home, he suffers the same fate from Ruth. But he keeps trying. "*Gaman*," he breathes to himself, hanging onto the words of his father: "Then no one can beat you!"

Ruth no longer cares about operating on snails and dedicates herself only to the practice of judo. It is all she wants to do. When she does judo right it is effortless. She can throw Hank over her hip or shoulder as if he weighs nothing at all, like a feather floating in the air. Judo is a wonderful mystery. She does not have a gi but fashions one from an old coat.

Kazu watches them practice.

"Ruthie. What about flower arrangement? Mrs. Kitigawa teaches the women Sundays after church. I'll take you."

Ruth sweeps Hank's leg out from under him. She turns to look at Kazu.

"I like judo better."

"Sure, okay," Kazu says.

He stares at Hank who still lies on the ground, blinking at the sky. Kazu's eyes turn dark with anger. "Are you dead? Then get up!"

Hank scrambles to his feet and stands hunched over like a small ape, his mouth half-open. They stare at each other. Hank seems to be waiting for his father to say more.

Kazu blinks. He studies something in the distance. He sighs. He nods as if in agreement with what he was looking at.

"Good ukemi, son."

Hank breaks into a grin. He pulls his gi into order and reties the belt.

"Let's go again!" he says to Ruth.

The summer is unusually warm. Their house does not have air conditioning, not even a box in the window. The nights don't seem much cooler than the days and sleeping is impossible. But Ruth thinks of something.

"Put your pillow on the floor, Hank."

"Okay."

"Now bring it back and put your face against it."

Hank does.

"Feel better?"

"Yeah."

On other nights she instructs Hank to sleep in the bathtub of their small bathroom where the porcelain is cool.

Hank vomits in the muggy, sweaty judo class. "Then I had to clean my throw-up from the mat," he tells Ruth when he gets home, and refuses to practice with her. The only tolerable activity is to play in the shade of the willow tree. The tree is large with long branches that hang to the ground and form a cool green cave. They climb the tree to sit on the limbs and sing songs, or fall into a silence until one of them notices something of interest from their vantage point, a stranger walking along the creek, an unusual bird drifting in the sky. Sometimes they break off thin branches, strip them of leaves and whip the ground and the tree trunk, then turn upon each other. Hank flicks his branch at Ruth's leg, but she steps back and whips his outstretched hand, making him cry. She goes to examine him. "Rub willow leaves on your hand. The pain is from a willow branch and the leaves will take it away." Hank does as she says. "It works," he says, sniffling.

Ruth is clever at many things. She teaches Hank to fashion a slip noose with a long stem of grass to catch lizards.

"Why don't they run away?"

"Because they see grass every day and it doesn't scare them."

They catch lizards in the woodpile, walk them like dogs with grass leashes, then release them.

There are two kinds of lizards. Alligator lizards are long and slender with black and yellow markings and tiny teeth no bigger than teeth on a file. They bite the children's fingers and Ruth and Hank laugh at how ferocious they appear but how little it hurts. The other lizards are blue bellies, with rough gray backs and smooth pale undersides streaked with color. These lizards never bite. Ruth shows Hank how to rub their bellies with a finger. The lizards fall into a trance and remain motionless until the rubbing stops, at which point they come to their senses, flip over, and scurry away.

Ruth catches a blue belly. "Watch." She pulls on the tail so it breaks off and twitches in her palm. A small drop of blood oozes out.

"It's moving!" Hank screams.

"It helps them escape."

"It's still moving."

"It tricks the bigger animal to eat the tail instead." Ruth does not know if this is true or not, but Hank seems to believe her.

She points to a lizard on the woodpile.

"That one lost its tail. The new part is a different color. See? They're not hurt."

"Can the tail of one lizard fit onto another lizard?"

Ruth turns away to fashion a grass noose as if she didn't hear.

The next day she says, "Let's do an experiment. Take the tail from one lizard and put it on another lizard."

Hank frowns. His dark eyes shift back and forth as if trying to remember something.

They catch blue bellies in pairs, paint numbers on their backs using twigs and an old can of primer. The same number goes on the tail. Carefully, they detach the tails, switch lizards, and wrap the tail from one onto the other with white medical tape before letting them go. The tape comes off, but Ruth figures out how to wind rubber bands around to keep everything in place.

Each day they will catch lizards to see if the tails grow. In her pamphlet she will describe what they discover. Hank wants to name the lizards, but Ruth says, "Numbers are better than names because numbers are more exact."

"But each will have a different name."

"The names might be too long to write."

Hank nods, realizing as usual that Ruth is the better thinker.

There is no change in the lizard tails they catch the next day. The segments have not begun to grow together. They rewrap the tails with tape and rubber bands and release them. The following day is the same.

"It's not going to work," Hank complains.

"It will work."

Another day passes and still there is no change. The broken ends of the tails they examine are scabbed and dry.

"It's not working," says Hank.

"Stop complaining!"

Hank sniffles and wipes his eyes. Ruth turns her back and hunches over to concentrate on writing her notes. She ignores Hank and he returns alone to their bedroom to read a comic book.

She writes in the pamphlet: *Lizard tails roots*. She rereads this section and is eager for the weekend, especially Saturday when Hank goes to judo class. "He's a big baby and gets in the way," she thinks, marking in her notes.

But Saturday comes and Alice rings the bell frequently. It is exhausting to do even this. She rings as loud as she can, feeling the impatience of gravity pulling her into the earth. She can see the fields from her window.

It doesn't matter where she is buried. A cemetery, or she doesn't care, they can dig a hole and drop her in the fields. All earth is the same, a sieve her body will dissolve and pass through one day as her spirit rises to Heaven. But she must faithfully wait. For now, all she has is the love of how Ruth appears like an angel and the feel of the child's hand on her arm.

When Ruth is summoned she makes lunch, which Alice does not eat. She brings her glasses of water. Hank is not there to help. Ruth waits patiently for her mother to nap so she can forget about the bell for an hour or two. When Alice finally does, Ruth goes to the woodpile and searches carefully, knowing how lizards blend into the wood, but there are none to be seen. Clouds drift, blocking the sun. What seemed a promising day without Hank, who complains and interrupts her experiments, has become a day when Alice summons her again and again, and now there are no lizards. She sits by the woodpile. She fashions a grass noose. The afternoon passes.

A blue belly creeps from the shadows, its tiny black eyes flicking. Ruth holds her breath as the lizard inches forward. There is a number two painted on its back. It crawls across the gray wood, dragging behind a tail wrapped in dirty white tape and rubber bands. A number one is painted on the tail.

For a while Ruth and the lizard wait on the other. The clouds open and the sun bursts through. The air warms and the lizard closes its eyes. It is the only lizard she might find that day. But one lizard is enough. She can still write her notes. Cautiously, hardly breathing, she extends the green noose.

From her mother's open window comes the sound of the cowbell. It jars Ruth and makes her clumsy. The lizard blinks and disappears into the woodpile. She puts a rock on her pamphlet so the wind won't blow it away, gets to her feet and hurries to the house as the bell clangs.

"I wish it would stop ringing forever and ever," she thinks. She hates the bell, having to listen for it all day, nagging at her, not letting her accomplish what she needs to do.

"Water, please," Alice whispers from her bed.

Ruth stares at her from the doorway.

"I got you water."

"It's gone."

"I get you water and it makes you use the bathroom, then I have to help you again. Now I have to get you more water?"

"I'm sorry. I'm thirsty."

She has never spoken to her mother like this before and now she cannot stop.

"I never get to do anything! I always have to bring you water or something else!"

Her mother is silent. Ruth waits.

"I don't need water."

"Oh my God," Ruth says loudly.

She returns to the woodpile. "If she didn't need water, why did she ring the bell?" she thinks.

But *Oh my God* she has said. Ruth squats by the woodpile. "It's all she'll think about now."

She returns to the house to say she's sorry for taking the Lord's name in vain. She walks across the patio, through the kitchen, into the living room, and stops.

Alice is crawling on her hands and knees in her old pink nightgown, pushing the tray with an empty water glass. Her limp hair hangs across her face and all she can see is the plastic carpet runner that she follows. She shoves the tray forward with one hand, moves up a bit, and shoves the tray forward again.

"Mom!"

Ruth kneels down.

"Get away," Alice says. She must concentrate.

Ruth reaches for the tray. Alice swats her hand.

Ruth steps back not knowing what to do. With a set jaw, staring at the floor directly in front of her, Alice scoots little by little into the kitchen.

"Mommy—"

Alice is at the sink. From the floor she reaches up to place the empty glass on the countertop, feels for the tiled edge and, gripping it, struggles to pull herself up. Finally, she stands.

"Mommy!"

It is as though Ruth is witness to a terrible, slow-motion accident. Alice fills the glass with water and sets it on the countertop. She lowers herself to the floor, then reaches above for the glass. Holding the glass so it does not spill, she places it carefully on the tray. Alice crawls from the kitchen on her hands and knees, pushing the tray. Ruth follows, bending forward, her hands outstretched and imploring. When Alice is midway across the living room, the front door bangs opens. Hank is home from his judo lesson.

Hank's eyes widen. He drops his gi and rushes forward to help. In his haste he knocks over the glass of water and it spills across the carpet. Ruth seizes the water glass and runs into the kitchen to refill it. Now she can make up for what she did wrong! She returns to the living room and kneels for the tray. Alice smacks the glass from Ruth's hand. Hank, not understanding, watches in amazement. The glass flies through the air to shatter against the wooden table where the family photographs are. Alice, Ruth, and Hank, as though a single creature in a spasm of grief, burst into tears.

Chapter Three

THERE ARE Japanese American clubs for everything. Not only for Japanese arts and language, but for American activities. There are Japanese American Cub Scouts, Japanese American Boy Scouts, Japanese American chess clubs, Japanese American churches. There are Japanese American festivals and Japanese American beauty pageants where Japanese American girls from all over Los Angeles compete against each other in friendly events. When Hank enters the sixth grade, Kazu signs him up for the Japanese American Sports League. It is a dream come true for Hank. He finally gets to show Kazu and everybody else in the community what he is made of.

It is the end of July and Los Angeles is baking under the heat. Car exhaust from ten million cars pushes inland against the San Bernardino mountains, finds no outlet and hovers across the city in a brown cotton haze. Pop Warner football season is about to begin and so, too, the Japanese American Sports League. Each boy receives a box with a new helmet inside. Hank cannot put his down. Blue, gold and shiny. He wears it around the house, cradles it, sleeps with it in bed. Ruth is envious and wants to wear the helmet. Hank lets her, but grudgingly. He does not like her to wear his helmet, does not like the strands of hair or the smell of her head she leaves behind. She is a girl. Hank fears her substances will weaken him in the manly game of football.

The coaches are fathers, men Hank has known all his life. Silver whistles hang from their necks as symbols of authority. They blow the whistles, yell, command boys around the field. "Don't walk, run! Keep your knees up, head down! Push! Hit hard! Harder!" They bark instructions like the drill sergeants they once suffered under in the U.S. Army. Hank loves running and charging, pushing and shoving. And the drills. Hank dashes right and cuts left to leave the defender looking silly as he catches the ball and runs into the end zone. Hank loves the diagrams of plays, the swooping arrows indicating motion and trajectory. He loves the huddle, the terse calling of strategy, the guttural shout in unison and slapping of hands. How they break into position to crush the enemy.

Coaches toughen the boys up, criticizing them at any sign of weakness. It doesn't matter what, running out of breath during sprints, falling down from a head butt, complaining of a finger in the eye, limping from a twisted ankle. If the boys don't push themselves until they feel sick the coaches accuse them of not giving their all. The boys don't grumble. They know better. The coaches sound like their own fathers at home, encouraging the boys with only one word: *gaman*. Don't complain, endure, accept the pain, tough it out. Each boy grew up hearing *gaman*, *gaman* from their fathers until the boys believed it was the only thing that mattered. For their parent's generation, it was.

As the boys run around the field and throw footballs at each other as hard as they can, the coaches are watching. They bend their heads together, confer and write notes on their clipboards. The boy they choose for quarterback is James Inouye, the boy everyone knew it would be. In elementary school his athleticism was apparent to all. Among the crowd of children running on the playground he alone appeared as a loping animal, a gazelle or leopard. He made hopscotch and four-square look effortless and beautiful. He was feared in the tetherball circle for smashing the yellow ball so hard that stopping it hurt the hand. He moved with the grace of a boxer in dodgeball, never getting hit, and yet no boy escaped his aim. Being struck by a ball James Inouye hurled felt like being struck with a bat. James has two friends, Ed Ueda and Noah Yano, and the three are inseparable. They are known as the Three Kings. Every school has boys that outshine the others, and sometimes they are hated, but each of these Kings are mentored by their parents in the benevolence expected of royalty. They are worshipped. The girls discuss the merits of their faces and hair, the boys wish they could be one of them. Not be like one, but be one, willing to trade their lives, their personalities, their families, for a better existence. It is no surprise that James is chosen as quarterback, with Eddie and Noah as halfbacks. For the rest of the team, the coaches let boys try out for any position they wish to play.

Hank picks offensive end. He wants to catch the football and run into the end zone. He imagines Kazu and Ruth in the bleachers watching him repeatedly score and his team cheer him on as he carries them to victory. He imagines the Three Kings accepting him as a friend. Being friends with the Kings will assign him favor in the community and make his father proud.

To strengthen himself, Hank begins doing push-ups. Each day he will do twenty-five. But they are more difficult than he imagined, and he drops down to twenty, then fifteen, then ten. After that he decides they are unnecessary. Offensive end requires speed, not big muscles. The coaches show them how to toughen up their guts by punching themselves there with their fists. When Kazu is around, Hank pounds on his stomach especially hard, as though it is nothing! Kazu watches and grunts with approval.

The coaches think Hank's small size means speed and quickness. They clap him on the shoulder, swat his helmet to rattle his head, and shout, "Show us what you can do!"

But as practice moves from drills to scrimmage, it is clear Hank has neither speed nor quickness. Worse, he has trouble catching the ball. It flies through his arms, or bounces off his chest. When someone suggests gloves, he brings an old pair of Kazu's gardening gloves to the field, but it makes no difference. He misses perfectly thrown passes so often the coaches move another boy into his spot.

"Try defensive end," they tell Hank. "Stay close. Don't let him get away!"

The boy he is supposed to guard is too fast and leaves Hank behind. Hank cannot keep up with anybody.

"Hmm. You're small, but try the line. Get in there!"

Hank lowers his head and pumps his legs furiously, but never gets past anyone. As a defender Hank is easily brushed aside.

When the season begins Hank is placed in last string along with several others.

"You boys are our secret weapons. Rest, be ready for when we need you. Chins up! It's possible you can save the game!" the coaches tell them.

They sit on the bench. Occasionally they are called upon during the last ten minutes of games with such lopsided scores it does not matter either way. "Tanazaki!" they shout, and Hank jumps to his feet. Pulling on his helmet he rushes to the field, looking quickly to the left, then to the right, assessing the situation. From the stands Ruth waves both arms. Hank pretends not to notice. He glances at his father.

Kazu stares and gives him a nod.

The season draws to a close. The Three Kings take their team to the championship game against Crenshaw. The Crenshaw quarterback is Filipino, a boy everyone calls RB, one of the best junior athletes in all of Los Angeles. There is grumbling about his race, but Crenshaw claims he has Japanese blood from a romantic encounter in the cane fields of the Big Island a generation or so ago. Rules that govern this kind of thing have not yet been established by the Japanese American Sports League committee. The boy, RB, is the reason Crenshaw is favored to win. But victory does not depend on one player alone, and under the pressure of a championship game, his team falls to pieces. In the last ten minutes of the fourth quarter Hank's team is ahead by 36 points, a slaughter.

"Tanazaki!"

They have the ball on the five yard line at their end of the field. Hank leaps off the bench and runs quickly, aching to show his worth. His breathing is raspy and loud in his helmet and the green grass and white chalk lines fly beneath his feet. The center snaps the ball. Inouye hands off to Yano for an end run. A defender hits Yano so hard the ball flies from his hands to the ground. Hank is there, so close it seems planned. The oblong brown ball tumbles to him in jerky bounces. He scoops it up, knowing he must first run back, away from the swarming enemies in different colored jerseys, then to the side and around to the open field. But he is tackled holding the ball in his own end zone. The other team is awarded a two-point safety.

Everyone laughs about it afterwards. They won the game easily and Hank has given them something to talk about for years to come. No one is mad. They punch his arm and make jokes.

"Give him the ball and he'll get in the end zone!"

"But the wrong one!"

When they get home, Ruth tells him, "Hank, you almost got away. You would have been in the clear and made a touchdown."

"I wish there was another game. Just one more!" Hank punches his fist into his hand.

Their father enters their bedroom. Hank looks up expectantly. "Put your helmet in the box so I can return it to Coach," Kazu says, and waits for Hank to do it.

Basketball season begins. The coaches teach them rudimentary aspects of the game, they explain each position in a sentence or two and encourage the boys, but that's about all. They saw during football season that boys are generally either already good or already bad, and in the short run no amount of coaching is going to change it. Hank tries as hard as he can, but quickly filters down into last string. The same last string football boys are with him again, and Hank imagines they will be friends. But the boys fear the other players will invent names for them. Team Slow Pokes, Team Bench, Team Baka, and they remain distant from each other. To target an individual is cruel and unsportsmanlike, but the anonymity of a group would allow them to be ridiculed.

The coaches send in benchwarmers frequently. They get to play at least five or six minutes every game. Hank likes how the waxed floor gleams under the bright lights, how the ball slaps and echoes and makes the floor tremble, and how the shouting of spectators in the background as he takes to the court makes him feel that everything depends on him. Each week a team letter, written by one of the mothers, is printed and distributed. There is always a column to celebrate players. The Three Kings take up most of the column and then the other two first-string players. The rest are given space appropriate to their standings, and benchwarmers are mentioned last with a general sentence for each. Lancelot Yamada tried hard! Lincoln Hashimoto got a rebound! Hank always looks for his name.

Toward the end of the season, Ruth runs to him waving the newsletter in her hand. She points to a sentence.

Hank Tanazaki has improved his dribbling!

Hank reads the words over and over, his lips moving silently. He hands the paper back to Ruth, saying nothing. He leaves the room.

"You're improving, Hank!" Ruth follows behind.

There is something about Ruth's face, how eager and kind it is, her smile of crooked teeth, her thick eyebrows raised in appreciation.

"Don't be so stupid," he says.

Ruth blinks and lowers her eyes. Hank watches her walk away, tall and skinny in her blue checkered dress, her mop of black hair growing back from Kazu's last haircut. Later, Hank tries to be friendly, but she avoids him.

Baseball season arrives. It is Hank's final chance. Other last string boys no longer care about trying or being made fun of and they fool around during practice. But Hank is determined. He asks Alice if prayer will help. He kneels at her bedside and closes his eyes as his mother prays.

"Dear Lord, please help Hank do well in baseball. Let his skills improve and let him find guidance and your glory. In the name of Jesus Christ. Amen."

"In the name of Jesus Christ. Amen."

Hank leaves Alice's room feeling that a spirit has entered his body and taken possession of his limbs. At practice he flies around the bases, catches fly balls and quickly snaps them to the infield. From the corner of his eyes he sees the coaches notice.

One day the coaches show the boys how to bunt. Right away, Hank knows it is the technique for him. He isn't big and he lacks power in his swing. But the bunt does not require power. He can get on base. If he can get on base he can score or help another boy score. When it is his turn to try, he grips the wooden bat exactly as the coach demonstrated, but when the pitch comes the ball smashes into his fingers instead of the bat. He drops the bat and clutches his hands between his legs. Hank's fingers swell, turn black and purple, and he cannot close them for a week.

After that he is scared of the ball. If a pitch comes fast or with a slight curve he jumps out of the batter's box. When the season officially begins he sits in the dugout with other last string boys. Their fooling around during games does not include Hank, for they had seen his efforts to improve and be better than them.

When the sports year is finished, Hank remembers the friendships he imagined forming, the pride in Kazu's eyes he wanted to see.

The end of the year team gathering is at James Inouye's house. Mr. Inouye is the community dentist children fear. He has a thin mustache and thick fumbling fingers that stretch their lips until the corners of their mouths bleed. Nor is he a good dentist for adults. Fillings fall out, caps must be reset, his Novocaine shots are administered so painfully it almost seems better to take the drilling without. But he fought with the 442nd and so everyone goes to him, grimly, like they had gone to the camps and the war.

A white cement path curves gracefully past large rocks among small trees, floating on a lawn that is neatly edged and so lush and green that Hank wonders not for the first time why his father, a gardener, cannot make their own yard look so nice. He works for rich people in Beverly Hills and must do a good job for them. Why not us? Ruth walks ahead carrying a bowl of potato salad she made.

Shoes are placed in neat lines around the entryway of the house and Hank adds his carefully. There will be slippers waiting for him on the patio. The Inouye house is not comfortable. It feels like church, where he must be quiet and not himself. He slides his stocking feet on the wood floor beneath the high ceiling of exposed beams, past paintings on the walls, along scrolls of black ink calligraphy. On glass shelves are vases, wood carvings, and ceramic bowls from pre-war Japan, Ruth informed him. The objects seem to be alive and watching him through generations of time, disappointed in what they see.

With relief, he steps onto a large cement patio that sparkles in the bright sun, where sounds of voices rise and fall in the warm afternoon air. Fathers gather in one group and mothers in another. He is not surprised to see the mothers wave at Ruth and call for her to join them. They know she is smart at school and gives up her social life to take care of their mother. Adults like that kind of thing.

From their tables, a few fathers glance at Hank, but neither wave nor acknowledge him.

At the opposite end of the patio and partway around the side of the house the team is gathered. He finds a pair of slippers and follows the shouting and laughter.

The boys on the team have known each other since they were little. They attend the same community picnics, the same Methodist church on Centinela Avenue, the same funerals and weddings. Hank sees them riding bikes together or reading comic books at the pharmacy. He overhears them talk about overnight sleepovers and so and so's mom who gives them frozen pizza and Coke floats. In the Inouye backyard the boys clump together, hopping up and down, jostling each other, hanging on each other, squirming and pressing in from all sides like grunion.

Looking on from the outskirts of the group is a squat, thick-shouldered boy it takes Hank a moment to recognize. Someone he hasn't seen for years.

"It's Tak," he thinks.

Everyone in the community knows Tak Nakamura. When he was younger Tak bullied smaller children. He'd hide behind a banana tree in his front yard and rush out like a monster to knock the smaller victims down. He once pushed Hank to the ground and pinned his arms with his knees and shoved a long stem of grass up Hank's nose. Hank screamed and Tak let spit drip from his lips into Hank's open, screaming mouth. It was such a success that Tak tried the same thing with an even smaller boy than Hank, but the boy was able to wiggle an arm free and pull a pencil from his shirt pocket and stab Tak's eye. Everyone was glad. The pencil lead made a small, round black dot in the white of Tak's eye like the mark of Cain. Tak disappeared after that.

Seeing Tak standing apart from the group, looking on with his shoulders slumped and his hands in his pockets, Hank is no longer afraid of him. It was a long time ago when Tak beat him up, and besides, Hank figures, it's just something boys like to do. Hank has also felt like doing it to kids smaller than himself.

"Hi, Tak," Hank mumbles.

"Hey, Hank," Tak says quietly. He looks at the ground, nodding his large head.

Hank nods with him in silence.

"Watcha been doing?" Hank says.

"Helping my dad wash windows." Tak shrugs. His once-roaring voice has become wistful, even sad. His black hair is long and oily looking.

"You should have joined the team," Hank says.

"Yeah, musta been fun. Real fun."

"It was," Hank says. "It was fun."

Tak grins. "I heard about your reverse touchdown."

"I felt stupid."

"It's just a game."

"Yeah."

"Hey, wanna have a…" Tak lifts two fingers to his lips and raises his eyebrows.

The small, perfect dot in the white of Tak's eye is still there. "Nah, I better join my team."

"Okay," Tak says.

The team is gathered around the Three Kings and someone makes room for Hank. He squeezes in.

"It's Hank!"

"Hey Hank!"

"He scored for the other team!"

"Hank, we didn't know whose side you were on!"

The boys laugh gleefully and turn their grinning faces upon him, even the Three Kings do. Hank feels pride at the attention. "I didn't know where I was," he shouts.

"He didn't know up from down!"

"What about when Yano made the interception!" As one, the boys turn from Hank to Noah Yano.

"Yeah, what a catch!"

"What a run! Twenty-five yards!"

"If I didn't get tackled I would have made a touchdown," Hank yells. But no one seems to hear. He hopes somebody will say something about him again, but no one does. The crowd of boys surge on without him.

After a while he backs out of the group and looks for Tak, but the boy must have gone home.

There is a chair in the shade of a small tree and Hank decides to get a plate of food. From here he can watch his father drinking with other fathers as they talk and laugh at jokes. Hank cannot hear what they are saying, but it must be the stories they think are funny, the same ones they tell whenever they get together and drink. How dumb to laugh at the same stories year after year. He watches as they drink, draining bottles of beer and sipping at glasses of whiskey poured over ice. Hank would like to try that soon himself, to see if drinking makes life funnier.

He munches on a chicken leg. Mrs. Inouye is famous for her chicken legs. Hank remembers a church picnic when Tak said, "Mr. Inouye sure likes Mrs. Inouye's chicken legs," and laughed like a hyena. Other boys heard him but didn't laugh. They acted like they didn't know what he was talking about and moved away. It was dumb how they were scared of Tak. Maybe Tak was dangerous once, but not anymore. "You know who is dangerous?" Hank would like to say, "Geoff Kimura, who stabbed the pencil in Tak's eye. He's good at math and he's in the Science Club at school. That's why he had a pencil. He's the one that's dangerous."

The women at the mother's table are turned to Ruth, who is smirking. Ruth does that when adults say nice things about her. She pretends she is not interested in hearing it, but Hank knows it is all she ever wants to hear. Ruth has a lot of dumb looks. Hank knows what each of them are and what they mean.

His father lifts a beer can upwards in a toast to something dumb, Hank is sure. The men point to bottles they want passed their way and puff on cigarettes, tapping ash into empty beer cans. His father does not smoke, but he used to. He stopped when Mom asked him to stop. It's another famous family story, this one of how their father quit smoking just like that, tossed the ciggy out the window of the truck and never smoked again, not even once. "Such discipline and commitment," his mom or Ruth say when they hear the story being told again for the millionth time. "It's the Japanese way," his father always adds. He means the discipline and commitment. *It's the Japanese way*, his father always emphasizes, his dark eyes flicking over Hank's face, as if those four words are supposed to change Hank's life. Hank sees the shadows of wheels turning behind those eyes.

A plane rumbles above and the men lean back in unison. Like a flock of birds, Hank thinks, or another kind of animal that does everything the same as each other. It's just a plane, Hughes Aircraft is not far away, there are lots of planes every day. Is this one different? Hank cranes his neck along with the men who have fallen silent, until one of them says something and the others nod and they go back to smoking and drinking, making jokes as if the plane hadn't been important at all. It must be about the war. It's always something to do with the war. The men enjoy themselves, laughing and drinking until something about the war comes to their attention that is not meant to be funny, and the conversation stops. The men sit quietly, until one of them sighs, or makes a joke, and like waking from a nap they resume talking. Once Hank overheard Dr. Kiyonaga say that men will never forget the war, the violence will never leave their bodies, it stays there and affects their minds. Hank took that to mean his father will always have to think about his wound and the colostomy. It's true, his father must keep it clean every day and be on the lookout for new products, like better gaskets and seals. How could someone forget something like that?

Hank has seen the colostomy. Reddish pink, circular in shape, and puffy. Hank thinks it looks like a smooth, raw meat donut. The surgeon made a mistake and put it where the belt for his pants goes. This causes a lot of problems, and sometimes his father wears suspenders, which look dumb. The colostomy can gurgle. When it does, his father laughs as if the colostomy told a joke. He says it gurgles less if he leans to the right, so he sits and stands funny, like he is leaning against a wall that isn't there. Sometimes it smells bad. Not that anyone cares. He got it from the war. Everyone in the community knows he has a colostomy. Some of the men here were in the battle and saw it happen.

The camps, the Po Valley Campaign, the Texas Lost Battalion battle where Kazu was wounded and his brother, Hank's namesake, killed. Hank knows the stories. They seem like the Bible stories his mother used to read him at night. Stories that mean something, but no one explains what. No one explains, but he is expected to know. As if their house has a hidden room he can never find. Ruth has been in the room and seen what is there and she knows what to do and say. But she won't tell him about it. To know without being told is what his father wants from him. But how can he know anything if no one will tell him?

The mail is delivered to a mailbox at the end of the dirt road. It is too early, but Hank goes to check anyway, just to get out of the house and away from the presence of his sister. Ruth no longer wants to do anything fun. She reads, prepares food, cleans the house, or simply hovers, taking up space and waiting for Alice to ring the bell. Then she drops whatever she is doing and rushes to their mother's room. In the past they exchanged looks of annoyance when the bell rang, Ruth rolled her eyes. But now she avoids looking at Hank when they hear the bell, her face expressionless as a mask. What is she thinking? Hank cannot tell. They wander past each other with nothing to say, or she asks dumb, adult questions: "What do you want to be when you grow up?" "Are you excited about junior high?" "What subjects do you think you will like best?" They don't talk like they used to. No longer do they take turns going to their mother's room when she summons them. Ruth doesn't give him the chance, she is always there before him, and he is not going to treat it like a race. Just because she didn't get a drink of water that day for Mom. Now Ruth is different. Who can do the most for Mom? If Ruth wants to take over everything, that is fine. There's no reason to stay home on the weekends and worry about their mother when good, dependable, boring old Ruth is here. Hank shuffles outside, remembering how he used to wait for Ruth to do all the thinking for him. Now he doesn't care. Everything she thinks about is dumb.

He closes the mailbox and hears someone call his name. It is Tak, yelling from the other side of Centinela Avenue. He lives in the housing projects a mile east.

"Hank!" he shouts again as cars pass between them.

Hank waves to him and waits.

Tak hurries across the street, his longish black hair flopping.

"Hey, what's going on?" Tak is out of breath.

"Checking mail. What's up?"

"I dunno," Tak shrugs. "Throwing rocks in the creek."

A fence was recently installed along the creek, but it is easy to climb over and walk down the steep slope to the water. Hank has climbed over many times. He resents the fence and enjoys trespassing. In a few smooth motions he pulls himself up the chain link, pausing to sight down the fence line, lifts his leg carefully above the few strands of barbed wire at the top, swings the other leg over, and jumps to the ground on the other side. He waits for Tak to follow. The larger boy has difficulty.

"Hold yourself up and lift your leg."

"I'm trying. Fuck. The barbwire."

Then he is over and hops down next to Hank. They descend carefully on the sloping bank. It is mid-tide. At the shoreline they look for stones to skip. Hank finds a good stone that is round and flat and skips it to the other bank. Tak is not very skilled. His stones hit the water at the wrong angle and skip just a few times before sinking.

"Hold it like this and get closer to the water."

Tak can throw hard but he cannot get the angle right.

"Aw, fuck it." He pushes his hand through his hair. He wears a black leather jacket with zipper pockets that make him look like a tough guy. Hank likes it but knows Kazu would never let him have one. The sun is overhead, the hot air motionless and stinking from the still, dirty water. Wearing a thick jacket in the heat does not seem to bother Tak. From one of his pockets he pulls out a pack of cigarettes.

"Wanna smoke?"

"Sure."

Hank has never smoked before, but he's not going to refuse. He puts a cigarette in his mouth while Tak strikes a match, cups it in his hand, and holds it to the end of Hank's cigarette. He waves the match and tosses it in the water. Hank inhales and coughs.

"Your first time?"

"Yeah."

"Fill your mouth first and then inhale, like this."

Hank does. It is sharp at the back of his throat but he manages to inhale without coughing.

"See?" Tak is pleased.

Hank does it a few more times.

"I feel dizzy."

"That's okay. You have to get used to it. Wanna sit down?" They squat on the bank.

It is the first time he has seen Tak since the team gathering at the Inouye house a week earlier.

"Why didn't you sign up for sports? You came to the party," Hank says.

"I crashed it, hehheh."

"The party?"

"I heard about it and went."

"You didn't come with someone?"

"Nah. That's what they all thought. Like, 'Who the hell brought Tak?'" He grins at Hank. His hair hangs partway across his wide face. "I came for the food. Knew there'd be good food. My mom don't cook much, only shit outta cans."

Hank is silent. He would not consider going to a party where he was not invited.

"Whatta you think about that?"

The soft spoken, modest voice Tak used at the team party is gone. He sounds more like the old Tak, the one who terrorized children, the one who shoved a stem of grass up Hank's nose and spit in his mouth.

Hank's cigarette burns down. He throws it in the water. He doesn't feel good. Tak takes a final draw from his and flicks it after Hank's. A mud hen breaks away from several others and hurries over to where the stub floats.

"Stupid bird," Tak laughs. "Nah, the sports league. I don't like that stuff. Why call it Japanese American Sports League? Why not just American? We're American, right?"

"Yeah."

"So? I'm American, you're American."

Hank shrugs. There's a reason they call themselves Japanese American, but he cannot remember why.

"That's what my dad says, anyway. Mom says they're getting back together, but I don't think so. He has a hakujin girlfriend with big tits. I met her. She's okay."

They toss rocks in the water. Cars pass on the Centinela bridge and a large truck rumbles across. A car honks and they look up as it speeds away. On the other side of the creek a small engine with a pipe that goes down to the water and a pipe that goes up the bank putters noisily. It pumps water from the creek into a tomato field on the other side.

Hank points to it. "My dad says the farmer gets free water."

"Free water? Shit, nothing's free. He has to pay for gas."

Hank does not think Tak can know more than his father, but it is true that gas costs money. The water is not really free.

Tak shakes out another cigarette and offers it to Hank.

"Okay."

They light up. Tak watches to make sure Hank is doing it right.

"Don't put the whole filter in your mouth, just the tip."

Hank nods.

"Let's check out the drain tunnel."

"Okay."

The entrance to the cement tunnel is large enough for a truck to drive through. A gate of metal bars hangs across the opening.

They peer inside. Daylight penetrates for several yards and grows dim. Beyond that it is pitch black. Knowing the tunnel extends forever beneath the city makes it seem even darker. Silence and cool air drift from within.

"They got these same big drains in New York City," Tak says. "Kids flush pet alligators down the toilet or throw them in gutters. But the alligators live and grow big, like in the swamp, and come out at night and eat small dogs and little kids."

The gate is hinged at the top. A thick chain and padlock secure the gate to a metal ring in the cement wall to keep it from swinging open.

"Look, they put the chain on too loose." Tak rattles the chain, he bends down and pulls at the gate until the chain stops it. Doing so creates an opening at the bottom.

"Go on," he says.

Hank hesitates.

"Hurry up! I can't hold it forever."

Hank drops his cigarette and lies down and scoots under the gate into the tunnel. Tak lets it swing back into place as Hank gets to his feet.

Hank looks back through the gate, past Tak, to the bright daylight and greenish water of the creek.

"You're in jail!" Tak grabs the bars of the gate and shakes it. "Go on," he says, waving his hand.

"What?"

"Go. Explore. See what's in there."

"You come with me."

"I can't hold the gate and crawl under at the same time. See how far you can push it."

Hank tries, but he cannot get it open enough for Tak to crawl under. Alone, with the gate no longer between him and the darkness, Hank is afraid. What Tak said about New York City could be true here. Ruth told him something lives in the tunnel. He clutches the bars of the gate.

"Haha, look at your arm."

Hank's arms are covered with goosebumps.

"My dad calls that chicken skin. You're scared!"

"I'm not!"

"I just thought of something. You can't get out by yourself."

"What?"

"You can't open the gate and get out at the same time. I have to help you."

Hank lies on the cold cement and strains against the gate. It is true, he cannot hold it open and slide under at the same time. "Come on, Tak," he says, looking up.

Tak does not say anything. He lights a cigarette and puffs a few times. He begins walking away. "Catch you later," he says.

"Tak!"

Tak laughs and comes back to pull the gate open enough for Hank to slither out.

They climb back over the fence and stand on the road.

"I have to get home," Hank says.

"How's Ruthie doing?" Tak calls her Ruthie like adults do.

"Fine."

"She's smart, huh?"

"Yeah."

"Go ahead, take one for later." Tak shakes out a cigarette.

"Thanks."

Tak pushes his hair back, gazing along the fence line and far down the road. "Next time I'll bring a piece of wood and block open the gate so we can both go in. I heard it goes for miles under the city. We'll climb out a gutter somewhere downtown. Imagine people at a bus stop, and all of a sudden we climb out the gutter!"

"Yeah."

"See you on the flip side," Tak says, pointing at Hank.

"Okay."

Hank walks the short distance home and goes into the kitchen where Ruth is.

"Where were you?"

"I went to get mail."

"I know. But you were gone so long."

"I saw Tak."

"Tak Nakamura? The one who used to beat you up?"

"Yeah. We threw rocks in the creek."

"Are you friends now?"

"I think so."

"You don't sound sure."

He stares at Ruth. "I'm sure!" he says.

Why does she question all the time? Irritated, he goes to the back yard and squats by the trash cans. As he puffs away on the cigarette Tak gave him, Hank remembers how his father quit smoking, just like that, flicked the cigarette out the window and never did it again. Discipline and dedication. He's made of the same stuff as his father. He can do it, too.

Chapter Four

THE WELL is not easy to find. Located between Loyola University and Hughes Aircraft, hidden by scrub brush and icicle plants that cover the hillside, it is an old well, the top welded shut since the accident. It should have been sealed when it was abandoned, but who could have known? When the well was dug it was in the middle of nowhere, long before Loyola University, Hughes Aircraft, before neighborhoods and houses appeared. Ruth is now fourteen years old and Hank twelve. It is 1964. Their bikes lay on the ground behind them. The funeral is tomorrow and they stare at the well and try to imagine what it was like for the boy who died there.

Joey Carson was not a friend, just a boy they knew from school and community picnics. He said hello in passing and did not stop to talk. But when they heard of his death he was suddenly illuminated. They remembered little things, how he helped a girl that sprained her ankle, how he cut lawns in the summer for his neighbors.

After the funeral service and burial, the Carson's house is filled with mourners wishing to pay respect to the parents and console the boy's sister, Shirley, who is Ruth's age. They bring food and drinks, but no alcohol. Emily and Tim Carson are devout Christians who do not drink. Being religious, they speak of Joey in present terms. They smile gently and nod, he is in a better place. Among the gathering is small group of boys and their families who keep to themselves and seem especially somber, even more so than the Carsons. These boys remain with their parents when the rest run downstairs into the back yard.

The younger ones find a swingset and little playhouse. Ruth and Hank stand off to the side of the lawn and talk with two girls whose parents are friends with the Carsons.

"He was there four days. He died of dehydration."

"But he was in a well," Ruth says.

"There was no water in it."

It didn't rain much during the winter and spring, and it is now the end of July.

"My dad said there was mud he tried to drink, but it made him sick."

"Did he fall in?"

"No, he climbed down with a rope, but it broke."

"No, he tied it to a bush and when he tried to climb back up it pulled the bush out."

"We saw the bushes," Ruth says.

"You went there?"

"Yes."

"Oh."

The two girls consider this. They hadn't gone to see the well and now wish they had.

"He wanted to join their club."

"What club?"

One of the girls makes a silent gesture, pointing with her finger up to the house where the group of boys are with their parents.

"He had to be accepted."

"An initiation."

"They threw something down the well. He had to go alone."

"What did they throw in?"

"It was a doll."

"No, a souvenir from a vacation."

"Why didn't they tell their parents?"

"They were afraid they would get in trouble."

"And then it was too late."

Hank listens and is silent. He could have been Joey, lowering himself down the well with a rope, thinking ahead to the faces of the boys as he showed them the thing they threw in there.

"The police said he tried really hard to climb out."

"There were marks on the inside of the well."

"But he couldn't get out."

That night Kazu made them sit with him at the kitchen table.

"The worst thing that can happen is to lose a child." Their father is so serious it frightens them.

Before he drifts off to sleep, Hank imagines being at the bottom of the well, looking up at the circle of blue sky, waiting for a face to appear.

The death of the young boy throws a dark mood over the community. The Carsons are well known. Emily is active in the church and Tim manages a Ford dealership in Crenshaw. Everyone knew Emily before the war when she was Emily Sato. The Carsons are a rare, mixed couple that others in the community gossip about. Not with malice, but with interest and mild concern. Tim is a tall man with blue eyes and light hair. Emily, half his height, is what people call a fireball. In Manzanar she organized volunteers to teach school, then a church group and choir where she also sang, and a fix-it team to repair cracks in the barracks walls through which sand blew in with the cold. After the war she was everywhere in the community, helping with paper drives, the O-Bon, church events, fundraisers for the Japanese language school. Emily was the sort of person who stands up first when volunteers are needed. She did everything asked of her, in addition to the task of raising her children. In public now, after the death of her son, she wears a smile on her face and is more enthusiastic than ever.

The summer passes. On new medicine, Alice continues to improve. She tires easily but cooks more often, sometimes three times a week. It is a great joy to the family. Kazu tried his best, but his culinary skills are small. Vienna sausages heated in the can until the jelly melts, then dumped over rice, Mulligan stew, and something called Shit-On-A-Shingle that Hank likes because of the name. But Alice makes teriyaki pork chops, sukiyaki, fish with shoyu and ginger, and other delicious foods seasoned with what she calls tasty salt, the little red tin of Ajinomoto on the stove. Hank and Ruth help her into the fishman's van when it comes down their dirt road twice a week. Inside, it smells as fresh as the ocean. The fishman wears a long, clean white coat, like a doctor, and black rubber boots. He displays wooden drawers of colorful fish with clear, bright eyes arranged nicely on ice. It reminds Hank of the donut truck and its drawers of glazed, jelly, sprinkled donuts and éclairs. But better than those are the ones Alice makes, sitting on a high stool at the stove, frying donuts in a Crisco can and dusting them with powdered sugar.

Ruth and Hank enter new schools. Hank to Marina Del Rey Junior High, and Ruth to Venice High. Of all the things to consider, clothes are the most important. Ruth spends hours thinking about clothes, looking through magazines to see what other girls wear, listening to her parents' suggestions with a straight face as if they made any sense. If Ruth must dress as her parents want her to, she will die. Hair is equally important. Can she rat her thin hair into a beehive like the Ronettes? She admires how sophisticated and dangerous it looks. She expects a battle, because Mexican girls like it as well. She finds photos of Caucasian girls with beehives and cuts them out to show her parents.

For Hank it is much simpler. All he hopes is that his father does not do as he has always done, which is to make Hank wear jeans two sizes too large for him, to grow into, a belt bunching up the slack around the waist and the cuffs rolled up so Hank looks like a farmer. Please, please, he prays. In the excitement of preparation Hank and Ruth become friendly again. She gives Hank suggestions about shirts from the Sears catalog and how to comb his hair.

A clothesline with an old sheet hangs between their beds. Ruth put up the partition when she began seventh grade at Marina Del Rey, as Hank is now. Ruth talks to Kazu in private.

"Dad, it's weird me and Hank still share the same room."

"What do you mean? Did Hank do something?"

"No! Dad, it's our ages."

Kazu nods. "Hmm. Okay."

At dinner that night Kazu makes an announcement.

"You kids are growing up. Going into high school, junior high school. It's time you have your own rooms," Kazu says. "Hank, now that you're a big boy, I think you will like the outside room."

Hank waits silently.

"Won't that be nice?" Alice says.

"Sure," says Hank.

The outside room is the size of a large closet, attached to the house but with its own door that opens onto the patio. To go into the kitchen, the small bathroom he and Ruth share, or anywhere else in the house, Hank must first go outside.

The room is dusty and crammed with junk. Broken lamps, bundles of magazines, a sewing machine, an empty aquarium, a chair with a broken leg, and other forgotten objects waiting for repair. When things disappear into this room, no one sees them again. Ruth helps Hank carry junk to the garage and a small shed in the back yard. All that remains is a bare lightbulb hanging from a cord in the middle of the ceiling. There are no windows in the room.

Ruth energetically sweeps and mops the old linoleum floor.

"I'll help you paint! We'll use bright colors!"

"Nah. It's good enough."

"It will make it so much nicer, Hank."

"It's fine as it is."

"Please let me."

"It's okay."

"Let me know if you change your mind."

"I will."

"Let's wash the walls!" Ruth exclaims. They soak rags in water but only smear dust and grime into fan-like patterns.

"Let's wash again," Ruth says.

"Nah, it's okay."

"I'll do it myself," Ruth says, and washes the walls a second time, but it doesn't do any good. Hank carries in his plastic models of Frankenstein and the Wolfman, but there isn't a window sill to display them. He places them in a corner on the floor where they threaten no one. He and Ruth stand back and survey the room.

"You can come visit me anytime you want," Ruth says.

"Okay."

"We're still in the same house."

"I know."

"It's a joke, Hank! Of course we're still in the same house!"

Hank nods and looks around the room. Later, he helps Kazu carry his bed inside, and they retrieve the small desk and chair from the storage shed where they had put them that morning. Both items are broken but still usable.

Kazu stands in the doorway. "What a nice room!" he says.

Hank sits on the bare mattress with his arms crossed and stares at the grimy, windowless wall.

"Make your bed and it will seem nicer."

Hank does not say anything.

"When I was your age, nine of us slept in the same room!"
Hank remains silent.
"At least you won't have to share your room with a girl!"
"Yeah," Hank says.

That night, Hank pulls and pushes on the door to make sure it is secure. He locks, unlocks, and locks the doorknob several times. At first he keeps the light on, thinking he might fall asleep that way, but the bare lightbulb is suspended above his face and when he turns his head to the side there is only a dingy blank wall to look at, or the chair with a broken crosspiece and the scruffy wooden desk. He switches off the light and gets back into bed, listening in the dark. Now he is glad there isn't a window for him to imagine something outside looking in. Hank wonders if Ruth is lonely in her room. When they were little, they lay awake after the lights were out and told funny stories to make each other laugh, or he'd ask Ruth about something and listen silently to her advice, knowing she is a better thinker than him. Sometimes Ruth snuck a flashlight from the kitchen to make animal shadows on the bedsheet between them. They had farting contests that Hank enjoyed, even when Ruth won, until Ruth lost interest in that competition some time ago. But the best thing was how they talked. The sound of her voice, like a friend in the dark, comforted him until one of them fell silent and both drifted off to sleep.

Wearing pants that fit, black dress shoes, a plaid shirt from Sears, his hair trimmed by Kazu into a little wave held in place by Butchwax, and a face shiny from scrubbing with hot water, Hank steps into the outdoor hallways of Marina Del Rey Junior High School. He is swept along by shrieking bodies and a sea of bouncing faces. He recognizes a few boys he knows from elementary school, the sports league, or his short-lived judo training. But no one stops to talk, sometimes a hello and a nod, but that is all. No matter, he is happy to be here, lost in a crowd, like ants passing and touching antennas, moving on to touch others. To be here among them all.

In first period he sits in the front row, as Ruth advised. But he has to keep twisting around to see who else is in the classroom. In the next class he moves to the middle row. Throughout the day he notices the last row is always filled with physically larger boys who lean their heads back against the wall and gaze upon the rest of the class with bored expressions. He sees a smaller boy sit in the back and a larger boy stand beside him until the first boy moves and the larger boy take his seat.

In physical education he is assigned a locker and learns about showers, getting a clean towel, and jockstraps. The school store next to the lunch area sells jockstraps. The boys are expected to have them by the next day. The PE teacher gives them a talk.

"Boys, the size of the jockstrap is for the size of your waist, not anything else. If you don't have a tubby size waist, like Lunch Box here," he points to a fat boy and there is laughter, even the boy laughs, "then do not ask for a size large. Every year we run out of size large because seventh grade boys think if you buy a large it means you're a ladies' man. Boys, you aren't, and you never will be. So get over it."

After school Hank stands in line at the student store. A tall girl with blond hair tends the counter. She eyes each boy with a bored expression as they step forward.

"Jockstrap, please."
"Size?"
"Large."
"Next."
"Jockstrap, please."
"Size?"
"Large."
"Next."

"Jockstrap."
"Size?"
"Extra large."
"We don't have extra large."
"Large, then."
"Next."

It is Hank's turn. The blonde girl at the counter wears pink lipstick and a pale, rose-colored sweater. Without meaning to, Hank stares at her breasts, then upwards to where she gazes at him with dispassionate green eyes. Hank has never beheld such beauty and sophistication.

"Next," she repeats, impatiently.

"Jockstrap, please," Hank says.

"Size?"

"Large."

She reaches for a box. "We are out of large. Only medium or small are left." She waits, her pink fingernails on the shiny metal counter go clickity-click.

Hank frowns. "Is there a medium-large?"

"No."

"Well, okay…medium."

She hands him a box with the medium jockstrap inside.

"Next."

After purchasing their jockstraps the boys run around the covered lunch area like they used to run around the playground in elementary school. The vice principal, an immense Black man with a bald head, dressed neatly in a powder blue suit and pink tie, appears.

"You all go home now. We'll see you tomorrow morning." His voice is deep, measured, and gravelly. His name, although students believe he made it up as a joke, is Mr. Nice.

Everyone calms down and leaves.

It is a short walk across the fields to school in the morning, and Hank arrives at a chaotic time as students slam their lockers shut and sprint to classes.

A girl rushes in late for first period.

"Well, it's Little Miss Muffet, sat too long on her tuffet," the teacher says.

In second period two boys hurry through the door, two minutes after the bell.

"Look who decided to join us. But the pleasure is not ours," the teacher says.

Teachers compete with each other to make clever insults. They are sarcastic and laugh at their own jokes. Except for Mr. Canetti, the social studies teacher, a tall, balding man with a longish, kind face. To latecomers he merely says, "Good morning." Or smiles and points to an empty seat.

After the last bell Hank leaves for home, wishing he could stay with other students as they form groups to run from one classroom to another and visit their teachers, or loiter in the lunch area where through a cafeteria window the lunch lady sells bags of potato chips, pretzels, and toasted bread with butter. Or venture onto the PE field where boys throw footballs and girls gather in small groups to jump rope, laughing and screaming.

Leaving the school and sounds of voices and laughter behind, he crosses the dirt field alone and goes into his backyard. He takes off his shoes at the kitchen door and leaves them on the patio, goes to his mother's room, and peeks inside to ask if she needs anything. If she is sleeping he backs away, retraces his steps to the patio, retrieves his shoes, and changes out of his school clothes in his room. Back in the kitchen he fixes a snack, pours water in a glass, quietly stirs in a spoonful of Tang, and eats a cookie. As he sits at the kitchen table he gazes absently at the closed door to Ruth's room.

When Ruth attended Marina Del Rey, it was her responsibility to take care of their mother after school and on the weekends. But it takes Ruth over an hour to walk home from Venice High, while Hank can be home in just a few minutes. It is fair: now is his turn to care for Mom after school. But what Kazu says at dinner that night bothers him.

"Ruthie, it's time for you to make friends and have a social life. You've taken care of Mom and now Hank can take over." Kazu glances at Hank with expectation in his dark eyes. "High school is the gate into college," he continues. "In college you meet a husband, a nice boy in medicine or law, both are good." His father makes it sound simple.

Ruth sighs. She pushes her meatloaf around the plate and across the table to Hank. He stares back but keeps his eyes neutral, not knowing what she wants.

"It's okay, then," their father concludes, "if you wish to stay after school, join a study club. Hank will be here. Find a Japanese American study club. That would be best."

In bed that night Hank imagines Ruth in a club, making friends, laughing, eating snacks at club meetings, being invited to someone's house for a sleepover. He wishes he could be in a club at school, though not a sports club. A study club. If he joined a study club he could meet friends. He would study hard, get good grades, and earn respect. Ruth will do it, Hank knows she will. Her life is going to change.

He lies in the dark, staring at the ceiling, wondering, "What about me?"

Chapter Five

Even if she were well, Alice would not go to church. Her idea of church is not a building. The real church is under a tree, by a stream, in a meadow, not the one down the street she made the children attend when they were little, the one they stopped going to the very day she said they didn't have to. And that is fine with Alice. The building with the gold-colored cross bolted into red brick was merely an introduction to a state of mind.

It is a state of mind she wants Ruth to understand about Saint Catherine of Siena. Hank is not ready to hear anything like this. It could disturb him. But Ruth. Ruth is different.

On this October day Alice feels well enough to walk around the yard and has asked Ruth to accompany her. The dying leaves of the willow are crinkly and falling away. The overcast sky brings a general coolness to the air.

They stroll past the lemon tree where a few leaves dangle from branches.

"I look forward to spring, when the tree flowers," Alice says, reaching out to touch a thin branch.

"The flowers smell so good," Ruth agrees.

They walk into the backyard. Alice points to a patch of tall weeds. "I had a garden there, do you remember?" Years ago she was strong enough to tend a flower garden. Camellias, chrysanthemums, hydrangeas, sunflowers, azaleas. Now just clumps of weeds. "When you were little we used to hold hands and walk between rows of hydrangea on tall stakes. You were so little the plants were like trees."

"I sort of remember."

"I heard a sermon on the radio this morning. Can I tell you?"

"Yes."

It is the reason for their walk. On Saturday mornings Kazu brings the transistor radio to Alice so she can listen while in bed, her Bible open, a pen and notepad at hand. Afterwards, if she feels well, she finds excuses to get Ruth alone and talk about what she heard. She doesn't care if Ruth questions or disagrees. In fact, Ruth's questions help Alice think more deeply. She knows Ruth does not believe any of it.

"Well, the sermon was very interesting and I thought of you. There was a woman, Saint Catherine of Siena."

"Where was she from?"

"Siena."

"Obviously, Mom. What country?"

"Italy."

"When did she live?"

"Oh, I can't remember. It was a long time ago. It doesn't matter."

"Mr. Mendez said it matters when people live, because time periods shape how people think."

"He is your social studies teacher?"

"Yes."

"Do you like him?"

"He's okay."

"You like high school?"

"It's okay."

"Have you met new friends?"

Ruth pushes her glasses up on her nose. "Yes."

"For some things it matters when people live. But other things are ageless. God is ageless."

"If God is ageless, he was always here. Why did he wait so long to make us?"

"That's a good question. I'm going to write a letter and ask someone from church."

By church Alice means a loose group of people who listen to the same radio show and occasionally exchange letters. Her most recent letter was to Edna, a woman who lives in Paoli, Indiana.

Alice wrote: *Dear Edna, My son Hank, twelve years old, likes the Beatles and wants to let his hair grow. He says Our Lord Jesus had long hair (which pictures show him as having). Should my husband and I let him?*

Edna, from Paoli, Indiana, answered: *Dear Alice, Would your son, Hank, atone for the sins of Mankind by suffering being nailed to the Cross? Can your son Hank rise from the dead? Our Savior, The Lord Jesus, is the Son of God and can do what He wants. Tell Hank to stop his foolishness and get a haircut. The Beatles? My goodness. They are girlish and dirty.*

Alice knows that Ruth wants to start an argument about God and agelessness and she is curious to know what Ruth will say. Nothing Ruth can say will bother her, because in the end it comes down to faith, and there is no argument against that.

But Ruth is silent. Alice reaches over and squeezes her hand. "Let me tell you what Saint Catherine of Siena did. She was a nun, who loved God. She helped poor people and practiced medicine."

"Was she a doctor?"

"No, but she tended to soldiers whose wounds were infected with gangrene. Imagine the rotting flesh, the blood, the pus, the smell."

"It sounds horrible."

"Yes, but what horrified her more than the blood and pus, more than the stink of rotting flesh, were her own feelings. The wounds repulsed her and she was ashamed of herself for feeling that way."

"But it's natural."

"For most people, but she was a servant of God. She pledged herself to serve Him. And yet she was unable to serve with unconditional love."

"Did God give her strength?"

"That's a good question. Did God give her strength, or did she find strength within herself to serve God? I'll write a letter and ask."

"Did she keep working there?"

"Yes. Saint Catherine of Siena did not run away from her service. Instead, to punish herself for her feelings, she went to the soldiers and collected a cup of pus from their rotting wounds. You know what she did with it?"

"What?"

"She drank it."

Ruth stops walking. She closes her eyes and shakes her head. "No," she says.

Alice watches her daughter. "That's duty, Ruth."

After school on Wednesday, Ruth climbs the well-worn stairs to room 213, where a study group meets. It is not the Japanese American study group Kazu hoped for. Those girls have their own study group with friends from the community. There was talk of including Ruth, but the girls think there is something odd about her. She is nice, but standoffish. At school they say hello to her, but conversation is awkward. "She thinks she's better than us," one of the girls says, and so Ruth is not invited.

The study group in room 213 is sparsely attended. Ruth recognizes a few girls from classes who glance at her, then away. No teachers are present. Most students sit by open windows to wave and yell at friends below, or gather around tables laughing and chattering, their books pushed to the side. Looking around the room she sees a girl sitting alone, watching her. The girl raises her hand, smiles, and waves for Ruth to come over. It is Shirley Carson, the girl whose brother Joey died in the well.

In all the years they've known each other, Ruth cannot remember saying more than a few passing words.

What Ruth knows most about Shirley Carson is how popular she is. It started in junior high when Shirley developed breasts before anybody else and the boys appeared to have never seen such things before.

As they chat about school and their classes, Ruth thinks how pretty Shirley is. Her hazel eyes have blue specks in the afternoon sun. Her black hair is ratted into the beehive Ruth wanted but was not allowed. And breasts. Ruth is tall and skinny, with a flat chest that makes her feel like a wooden plank someone hung an old dress on. Shirley wears a short skirt and moccasins. Ruth glances around the room wondering if other girls are comparing them.

They both have Mr. Mendez. "He seems nice," Ruth says.

"Do you know," Shirley says, leaning forward to whisper, "Mr. Mendez is having an affair with Miss Parker, the ceramics teacher."

"I thought he was married."

"He is."

"How do you know?"

"A girl I sit next to in class told me."

"Do you think it's true?"

"Her sister graduated last year and said everybody knows. Someone saw him coming from Miss Parker's room with his hair messed up and lipstick on his face."

Ruth likes Mr. Mendez, he makes social studies interesting. He invents stories about people in the past and how their lives must have been. He jokes and makes fun of students, especially the boys. Now she isn't sure. To do something like that, to treat his wife that way.

"He's old, he must be thirty, but awfully cute. I wouldn't mind." Shirley says, grinning, showing her even, white teeth.

It's not what Ruth expected Shirley to say. It must have shown on her face because Shirley stops grinning.

"I'm only kidding," she says.

"I know," says Ruth.

"But he does seem like a nice person."

"You never know about people," Ruth says.

Shirley opens a book and begins to read.

Ruth is unused to gossip. Anything people say or do out of the ordinary shocks her. It was for just a moment and now she has recovered, but she knows it is too late.

She watches Shirley read.

"I was sorry about Joey. I didn't tell you then. But I am sorry."

"Yeah," Shirley says, running her finger down a page.

During the service, Ruth thought about was how easily it could have been Hank. It was something Hank would do, something dangerous and stupid to impress other boys. But it wasn't Hank, and that it wasn't her brother gave Ruth a feeling of lightness. She couldn't help it. Ruth didn't talk to Shirley at the funeral service because she was afraid Shirley would see how she felt.

Ruth opens one of her books and pretends to read.

"They didn't even like Joey. Those boys," Shirley says, looking up.

"It was a club initiation, they must have liked him."

"They only told him to do it because they thought he wouldn't."

"But they threw something in the well for him to get."

"They didn't throw anything in the well."

"It was doll, or a souvenir."

"That's what they said, but it's not true. He went down there for nothing."

"Why would they do that?"

"I don't know. Fucking Japs."

Shirley returns to her book, eyes flicking across the pages. Ruth pretends to read for what she thinks is the right amount of time and then says she has to go home.

In the evening Kazu asks Ruth if she is okay.

"Yes, just so tired. I have a lot of studying to do."

Ruth goes to her room, closes the door, and lies on her bed.

In elementary school when a boy called her a Jap, she slapped his face and dug her fingers into his eyes. The following day Kazu left work early to meet with Ruth and the school principal.

"She attacked him savagely. She could have blinded him."

Kazu, holding his gardener's cap in his hands, apologized to the principal and in a gruff voice ordered Ruth to promise she would never do it again. But once in the truck he was no longer mad. On the way home he looked over to her with what she thought was a smile. They stopped at the pharmacy and Kazu gave her money for an ice cream sandwich.

She learned to keep her head up when someone calls her names, accuses her of bombing Pearl Harbor, or informs her out of nowhere that atomic bombs were dropped on Japan to save lives. Or the most frustrating taunt of all, telling her to go back to Japan, a place neither she nor her parents have ever been. Each time, she struggles to restrain the violence she wants to inflict. She reminds herself that people who say those things are ignorant people, the children who say it are the children of ignorant adults. But she has never heard someone who is Japanese say that word with such hate.

Half-Japanese, she reminds herself.

Ruth stops going to the study group. She only went in hopes of meeting other girls who might become friends and now there is no reason to continue. When Ruth sees Shirley in the hallway during passing periods, she bends her head to look through the books she carries, or pretends to search for her locker. She is relieved they do not share any classes.

"Meeting new friends at school?" Kazu asks her.

"Lots," she says.

Three weeks later, sitting in the lunch area by herself among hundreds of other students, she feels someone standing beside her. It is Shirley.

"Hello," Ruth says, trying to keep a pleasant expression.

"I haven't seen you at study group," Shirley says.

"I can't stay for it."

"I've heard you take care of your mother."

"Yes."

"Why doesn't your brother help?"

"He does. He goes right after school."

"So you don't really need to go home. You skip study group because of me."

It feels to Ruth that no answer she has ever given is as important as the answer she must now give. The way Shirley looks at her, waiting for her to speak, is how Ruth imagines God must gaze upon the world, with impassive eyes that simply watch and wait to see what people will do.

"Yes."

"I'm sorry."

Ruth wants to take Shirley's hands in her own, but she resists. "I understand," she says.

Ruth goes to the next study group and the ones after that, to talk with Shirley, just the two of them.

They meet for lunch at a bench near the ceramic studio to see if the rumor about Miss Parker and Mr. Mendez is true. But all they learn is that Miss Parker leaves her room exactly five minutes after the lunch bell and walks briskly to disappear around a building by the parking lot. They wonder if they should follow, but decide not to. The days are cloudy with gray light, and boys roam in small noisy groups, sometimes stopping to visit.

Ruth knows the boys who appear during lunch are not there for her. It is Shirley they swirl around, standing like a single creature with three or four nodding, bobbing heads, shoving their hands in their pockets and grinning, rocking back on their heels. They barely glance at Ruth. Only now and then, as if wondering why she is there.

Ruth's hair is cut straight across her forehead and the rest falls limply to her shoulders. She wears plaid cotton dresses buttoned at the neck and brown shoes. Their eyes move over her without interest.

She does not like how Shirley acts around boys. When it's just the two of them they talk of serious things, their plans for the future, what they think about their families. One day Shirley reveals something so serious about her parents that she starts to cry. Ruth feels a direct contact with Shirley's mind, her soul, everything they say is understood instantly by the other, as if the emotions of their lives are the same emotions. But how different and false Shirley is in the presence of boys. She giggles at everything they say, turning her face upward with a smile. When they leave, the way she yells, "See ya," her voice rising on the last note, makes Ruth hate her.

Yet, after the boys are gone far enough away not to hear, they begin a critique of each one.

"Did you notice his Adam's apple? He looks like a turkey."

"Whoever cut his hair should be arrested."

"The one standing close to me, I think he forgot to shower after gym."

"I wonder if he brushes his teeth."

"The other one tags along like a dog."

"A wiener dog."

Then it is fun and Ruth is ashamed she ever doubted her friend.

Later, walking home from school, she recalls everything she and

Shirley talked about, remembers the boys that stopped to chat, thinks of what she will say the next time in response.

One day, at the end of lunch after the boys are gone, Shirley asks, "Why do you hunch over in front of boys?"

"What do you mean?"

"You hunch over. Like this."

Shirley draws her shoulders inward and sinks her head between them. She straightens up and looks Ruth in the eyes. "You look like Quasimodo. You should stop doing that."

When she gets home Ruth stands in front of the mirror and imitates what Shirley did.

She finds Hank in the kitchen.

"Do I hunch?"

"What's that?"

Ruth shows him.

"Do I?"

"I don't know. Did someone say that?"

"Shirley said it."

"How would I know? I don't look at you."

The next time she sees boys coming to talk she makes herself sit up straight and Shirley gives her a look of approval.

"Why do you put your finger on your face and drag it across your cheek to your mouth?" Hank asks her one night.

"What are you talking about?"

"Did you see it in a movie or something?"

"Show me what you mean."

He pantomimes a poor imitation of a gesture Ruth recognizes as one that Shirley does around boys.

Ruth lets Shirley weave a small braid in her hair. At school when they meet for lunch she takes off her glasses and puts them in her purse.

Once, she catches herself saying to the boys, "See ya!"

But there are times she can hardly bring herself to meet Shirley. She dreads how boys compare them. Ruth can see it in their eyes, how quickly they assess, their eyes flicking over her just once to capture her entirety. Like animals, knowing instantly what is good and not good to eat.

That weekend Ruth goes for a long, aimless walk along the dirt road by their house, walking in the direction of the ocean. The sky is overcast, a salt breeze against her face. She drags her hand along the chain link fence that wasn't yet there when she and Hank killed a mud hen to feed the mother cat. She remembers the two boys they fought. How she punched and kicked them and drove them away. Had she really done that?

She stops to throw a rock, tracking it through the air to where it splashes in the water. When they were little, she and Hank used to throw rocks for what seemed like hours. She threw rocks further than Hank until one day he far outdistanced her. Just like that. Ruth remembers the disbelief on his face as they tried again and again. After that, Hank let her throw first and tried to match the splashes her rocks made instead of beating her. It didn't seem special at the time, him doing that. It was the same as when they shared anything, a bag of cookies, a slice of cake, making sure the other got the same amount. There wasn't a reason for him to beat her just to prove he could. In those days Hank wanted to be with her all the time. He followed her around, leaned against her, obeyed her commands, sought her approval, looked for her when they were apart. He didn't want to throw rocks further than her even though he could, as if he'd caught up to her in a race but refused to leave her behind. She thinks of how they pass each other in silence now. Why did it happen? One day she realized it had been like that for a while. She doesn't know how other families are. She imagines normal families talk to each other. But how silent Hank is. She doesn't know why.

She thinks about Shirley Carson, imagines her friend's face, the blue specks in her hazel eyes that appear in the sun. The way Shirley laughs as if laughter were the most important thing in the world. She hates how boys pay Shirley so much attention and her hardly any at all. Ruth sighs. Is it a competition? At times it seems so. The misery that overcomes her then is a new sort of misery, worse than any other. Does she really think boys might like her as they do Shirley? How ridiculous she must appear in Shirley's eyes.

She turns her back to the wind and, walking home, trails her other hand against the fence.

In mid-December it is chilly and bright. Ruth and Shirley sit on the cold cement bench and talk in the intimate way they do when alone, leaning toward each other, paying attention to each other's words as though each word is a stone placed carefully in a path they are building. Girls pass by. They look at Ruth and Shirley as though seeing something new and unexpected. Ruth knows what it is. Shirley Carson is attractive and popular, and she is Shirley's friend.

In the following days, when boys gather around, Ruth is content to watch them fidget and twitch, not caring whether they notice her or not. She is no longer compelled to animate herself in ways that later make her feel foolish. Her new attitude, she knows, has made everything better. An obstacle has been removed from between them. She knows that Shirley knows. Ruth is glad they say nothing about it.

It is almost time for the holidays.

"What will you do for Christmas vacation?" Shirley asks.

"Read. Do things around the house. What about you?"

"We always go to Mammoth and ski."

"Sounds like fun!"

"We almost decided not to go this year, but Mom says it is especially important to go."

"Because of Joey."

"She said traditions see people through hard times."

"So you're going?"

"Yes. And I want you to come with me."

Ruth shakes her head no.

"My parents said it's okay. Please, please come?"

"I need to think about it. Ask my dad."

Ruth imagined spending the holiday break as always. Helping with Alice, cleaning the house. She looked forward to visiting the library. She likes ghost stories that take place at sea, biographies, books about animals, detective stories, poetry. She returns the limit of books the following week for ten more. Hank is more discreet with his books, he borrows only one or two he grows bored with and does not finish. The librarian, glasses hanging from a cord around her neck, fawns over Ruth and ignores Hank completely.

She expects Kazu will say no to Mammoth because of Alice. But he surprises her. "Three days? I'll give you money. Don't let them pay for everything."

"Okay, thanks." Ruth pretends it is nothing special, then goes to her room and does a little dance.

They must leave at five o'clock in the morning to be on the mountain in the afternoon. Shirley will teach her to ski. Ruth pictures herself flying across the snow in a pretty sweater, a scarf blowing behind. Boys on holiday break from high schools all over California will be drawn to Shirley and gather around. Among them will be a boy, Ruth imagines, who looks at her in a shy way. If there isn't, well, she won't care.

Ruth has never been to Mammoth or anywhere else. She prepares herself, imagining how she will fall in the snow and look like a fool and she must laugh about it. If there is only one bathroom in the cabin what she will do if her stomach problems arise. Having dinner with Mr. and Mrs. Carson, searching for things to say. Ruth decides, if asked about Christmas, to lie and make something up. Alice considers Christmas a false celebration, a department store trick to get money, and they couldn't care less about Jesus! Ruth worries

Shirley's family will think her family is weird. She will not reveal that in secret she and Hank have exchanged gifts for years. Small items, a pair of socks, a cheap bracelet from the pharmacy. It is their way to celebrate, leaving gifts under each other's beds. She won't tell the Carsons her family does not even have a Christmas tree.

She and Shirley make preparations for the trip. Shirley has extra snow clothes and sweaters and scarves. If they don't fit she knows who she can borrow from. Shirley shows Ruth how to bend her knees and shift her body weight while skiing, demonstrating on a strip of grass near their bench at school. A boy in passing asks if she is teaching Ruth how to surf. Ruth wonders about skiing equipment. Shirley says boots and skis are available for rent. Ruth tells Shirley that she will pay for the equipment herself.

They leave for Mammoth on the first Monday after school lets out. Ruth cannot sleep. Normal families take vacations, normal families show their children the world. The furthest outposts of Ruth's world are Venice High School and the Mar Vista Library.

That weekend, Alice has a relapse. She was doing well and now she cannot get out of bed. Kazu pulls Ruth aside.

"Don't worry. It's only three days. Hank will be here."

Ruth walks on the road along the creek, letting her fingers tap across the chain-link fence. When she has a problem to solve, her thoughts never arrive in a reasoned order. Instead the answers appear as though they had been there all along, only needing to be uncovered and prodded awake. It is okay. Her father says it is. Hank will help with Alice. But the answer she finds is the one that was there before Shirley invited her, perhaps before she met Shirley. She is not surprised to find it waiting. The fight within herself from when she was younger is over. It's been over for a while.

She returns to the house to call Shirley and say she is sorry for the late notice, but she is no longer able to go.

Chapter Six

Mackerel skies. Hank looks at the clouds as he walks, remembering what Miss Crown told them in Science. Mackerel skies foretell a change in weather. *Mackerel sky, mackerel sky, never wet, never dry*, she said in a singsong voice they later made fun of. David made the most fun of Miss Crown and he is her favorite student. He has straight A's and always compliments her hair and what she is wearing. In the hallway outside of class he said, "She can have my mackerel!" Hank laughed, then looked around nervously.

Hank likes the cooler weather of winter, a chance for storms and lightning. He remembers the year it hailed, tiny white dots bouncing on their lawn. He'd never seen anything like it. He and Ruth rushed outside to gather a bowlful they put in the freezer and took out every now and then to examine until the little balls shrunk and disappeared.

Hank wanders around the neighborhood, walking here and there aimlessly. He goes to his old elementary school and peers at the empty buildings, remembering the past and visualizing himself running and playing with other children. There was a girl in the fourth grade he stared at all day long. She was blond with long wavy hair and blue eyes. Hank followed her home, stopping when she stopped to turn and stare back at him, continuing forward only when she continued forward. He wrote her a note: *I think I like you*, and gave it to her in class. The next day she told him, "I showed your note to my dad. He said stop writing me notes and stop following me home." Hank was crushed by those words and her remorseless eyes.

Here are the windows of his sixth-grade classroom where they heard the news that President Kennedy was assassinated. The teacher left the room and went into the hallway and laughed. Laughing so loud the children looked at each other in alarm. It wasn't until later he learned it wasn't laughter at all but crying and weeping. In the same class on a different day he had a vision. His penis rose from his pants to hover at the ceiling above his classmates like a giant worm, then swooped down and hugged a girl who sat on the other side of the room. He watched it coil around her shoulders like a boa constrictor. She didn't seem to notice and continued with their lesson in cursive. He was amazed and proud of his power.

Next on this day, under mackerel skies, he finds himself at the junior high school. It is closed for winter vacation and the athletic fields are deserted.

He walks through the parking lot and wonders what it is like inside the empty school. He can climb the fence, but it is very high and there he will be, twenty feet in the air in plain view. But here is an opening at the bottom of a wall that is large enough to crawl through. He glances over his shoulder and does not see anyone. In just a few seconds he is inside the school.

How strange and different being the only one here! He walks quietly in the outdoor hallway, alert to the slightest sound. How quiet, so quiet he expects to hear a footstep or a shouting voice any second. But no, the silence persists, and he relaxes. Here is his Math classroom, there is the hallway to his Social Studies class. Metal lockers line the walls. Hank tries several lockers, turning the black dials randomly, his fingers sensitive to any click. But he cannot open even one. He visits his own locker and spins the dial to unlock it.

There is nothing inside but an old sweater, too warm for the day he wore it. It lies crumpled in his locker, abandoned. Hank studies it, unsure why. He shuts the door to leave it in the dark. He walks through the entire school, his school. He owns it because he is here now when no one else is.

The covered lunch area is vast and still, silent as a cavern, the rows of empty tables, the cafeteria windows shut. He wanders to the athletic field, walking through the girl's side where they stand in rows during P.E. and chant, *We must! We must! We must build up our busts!* while stretching their elbows back to help their breasts grow. He walks around the gym office, peering through windows, then walks under the bleachers to see if he can find money. He heard someone found a dollar in change there. He takes care not to cross spaces where he might be seen from the other side of the fence, where the street and cars are. Feeling like a solider, or a spy, he stealthily makes his way back into the main part of the school and down a lane. Here is the entry to the Garden Club. His social studies teacher, Mr. Canetti, is the mentor and champion of the Garden Club. He tells the class how much fun it is to dig, plant seeds, water, and see the first green shoots appear. This year they will hold a fundraiser to build a greenhouse and a barbecue pit. There will be a wonderful party at the end of the school year for all members of the club to gather, cook hot dogs on the new barbecue, and eat salad made from what they grew. When Mr. Canetti talks about the garden club his eyes brighten and he radiates happiness. Hank lifts the latch on the gate and strolls around the garden. The greenhouse and barbecue pit have not yet been built but the fundraiser is soon to come. Here are the growing beds where students have prepared. He squats down and touches the dirt. He wishes he could be a member of the garden club. If he could, perhaps Kazu would be proud that he is taking care of plants. But the garden club meets after school and Alice is waiting at home. Squatting there, gazing at the mounds of dirt where little green shoots will soon appear, Hank decides to donate his allowance, the four dollars he receives each month for doing chores, to the garden club. "Every little bit helps," he thinks. He has never done anything like that, contributing to a common cause. It will make him feel good, being part of something bigger, part of a community.

Later, back at the house, he checks the little metal box where he keeps his allowance. He lost the key to it months ago but it doesn't matter, a paper clip works just as well. It is empty, but this Friday is allowance night and he'll have the four dollars then. He smiles at the thought of Mr. Canetti's face as he hands him the money. "What is this, Hank?" he imagines the teacher saying. "It's for the Garden Club. It's my monthly allowance, all of it!" Hank smiles again. Then he looks again into the empty metal box. After Monday, when he goes to school and gives his allowance to Mr. Canetti, it will be empty once more. For a month. Well, forever, if he contributes every month. Hank no longer smiles. Now he is worried. He will give a dollar each month instead. That seems better. Only a dollar. But after four months he will have given away the same amount that he earns in an entire month! Hank thinks harder. There must be something other than money he can give. He can sweep the sidewalk by the Garden Club. Kazu says that anyone can give money, but giving your time is even better. Hank returns the box to where he hides it in the pants drawer. It will feel good to help out the Garden Club.

The next day he walks to the record store where he likes to go inside and look at posters of the Beatles and other groups. It was here that Ruth bought a record, "The Monster Mash," by Bobby Picket and the Crypt-Kickers, and put it under his bed for Christmas. He goes into the TG&Y to wander around. There are a variety of things. Mattresses, kitchen tables, easy chairs, lamps, and framed artwork. There are rows of clothing for men and women and shelves of toys and board games. On the wall behind a glass counter are guns. Hank goes up and down the aisles, looking. Afterwards, he sits on the short wall of a small brick planting area where nothing is growing. Only cigarette butts and trash scattered in the dirt.

Someone comes from the Alpha Beta grocery. It is Tak. They haven't seen each other since smoking cigarettes at the creek.

"Whatcha been doing, man?" Tak says.

"Hanging around."

"I'm visiting my dad. You should come over to his place with me. I got my own room."

Tak wears a black leather jacket, the same one he wore at the creek. His longish hair falls across his face. He reaches in his jacket and takes out a short chain, the kind used to lock bicycles.

"Check this out. In Long Beach where my mom is you got to have something, man. It's rough over there."

Hank hefts the chain. He swings it through the air as Tak watches.

"No, man. Not like a cowboy. Someone will grab it. Like this." Tak wraps it around his fist and flicks the chain in quick motions at an imaginary head. "Take that, and that, and that!" He looks at Hank, grinning, and jerks his head at the TG&Y. "Is this the hot spot? This place is boring."

"Yeah," Hank agrees.

"You hungry? Let's get a burrito."

"Okay."

They walk a few blocks, cross the railroad tracks, and go past a Catholic church to a Mexican grocery store. A woman stirs a large pot of beans that smell delicious. She scoops some onto tortillas and wraps them up. Tak takes a roll of bills from his pocket and pays. They go outside and sit on the curb.

"You like your school?" Tak says.

"Yeah. You like yours?"

"I like the hot chicks. I'm telling you, man." Tak shakes his head wistfully. "What about your school? Got hot chicks?"

"Yeah."
"Scoring pussy?"
"Sometimes."
Tak nods. "Me too. All the time."
They finish eating and sit on the curb watching cars go by.
"I found a way to break into my school," Hank says. "You wanna see?"
"Shoot. Let's go."
The school parking lot is empty and nobody is around. Hank crawls through the hole in the wall and Tak follows. It is a tight fit for the larger boy so he takes off his jacket and passes it to Hank, then squirms through.
"Fucking-A," Tak says. He spreads his arms in amazement, turning from side to side in the empty hallway. He punches a locker with a karate yell, "Ha!" and looks at Hank with a sneer. He laughs. "Some fucker messes with me, that's what I do. I knock 'em out!"
Hank is nervous at the loud noise Tak made.
"Be cool," Hank says.
"Be cool what? Why should I?"
"What if there's a janitor?"
Tak quiets down. They walk around the school. Tak jiggles the handles of lockers and peers through classroom windows and tries doors, but nothing is open. Hank shows him where his locker is. "Open it," Tak says. Hank does and they look at his sweater. "Now close it and spin the dial." Hank does. "Now watch." Tak carefully turns the dial back and forth. After a few tries he gives up and they leave and walk to the P.E. field. Tak starts to run onto the grass field.
"A car will see us!" Hank says.
Tak trots back to where Hank is.
"Let's try the doors to the girl's gym."
"Okay."
But they are locked.

There is a ledge in a cinder brick wall. They climb up and sit, looking around. Without asking, Tak hands Hank a cigarette. When they smoked at the creek Tak gave him a cigarette for later, but it made Hank dizzy. This time he only draws smoke into his mouth and blows it out again, hoping Tak won't notice. To distract him, Hank points across the dirt fields. "That's my house."

"That's your house? I knew you lived over there somewhere, but not which house."

"That's the one."

"The last one on the road."

"Yeah."

"The end of the road."

"Yeah."

"You know what that means, right? The end of the road."

"I guess."

"It means nowhere else to go. You're shit outta luck."

Tak looks at Hank.

"Just kiddin', man! Don't be so serious!"

"I'm not. I like it!"

They jump down and walk around some more.

"What's over there?"

"Nothing, just the Garden Club."

Tak starts to walk in that direction.

"There's nothing there, just dirt."

"Your school is boring. Boring. Boring."

They go to the outdoor stage. It is made of cement and is supposed to be for school assemblies but there hasn't yet been one. A flagpole is at each side. Without saying anything, Tak drags a trashcan to the flagpole. Hank watches, not knowing what to expect. Tak unwinds rope from the cleat and ties one end to a handle on the trashcan. Then he hoists it up. Hank watches the trashcan rise into the air until it reaches the top. Tak wraps the rope back around the cleat.

"I was an honor guard in the Boy Scouts." Tak stands back and give the trashcan a Nazi salute. "Heil Hitler!"

Hank looks around.

"Take it down and let's go."

"No way. It will be cool when school starts." Tak points upward. "That's our flag!"

Kazu pulls the truck over and gives Ruth a five-dollar bill. It is her first time to the ice rink. "I always wanted to ice skate. Never found the time," Kazu says. She can't imagine her father ice skating, something so frivolous and fun-looking. She finds a place in the small line at a window, pays and steps through the doors. The cold air inside thrills her. Skaters crowd around a short wooden wall that encloses the rink, talking and laughing with loud, cheerful voices. A machine with large spinning brooms nosily circles the ice.

She shuffles sideways through the crowd and climbs the steps at the far end of the oblong rink. The ice glows white beneath bright lights hanging from the middle of the ceiling. The machine continues its journey around and around. She didn't think cold has a smell, but it does. Music blares from speakers somewhere above.

Sitting a few rows from the top of the bleachers, she twists around to see what is above her. The top row is dark and couples are kissing, wrapped in each other's arms. She turns away.

Then looks back for a few seconds.

The machine finally exits the rink. Gates open and skaters spill onto the ice. Some hang on the short wall, venture forth briefly, then return to hang on the wall again. Others glide beautifully, some turning to skate backwards in long, relaxed strides. Their movements look effortless and free.

Ruth cannot wait to try skating. Then later they will sip hot chocolate while Shirley tells her about what happened at Mammoth. She studies the movements of skaters below, forming an idea of how they propel themselves across the ice. "I can do that," she thinks.

A figure is climbing the steps toward her.

Shirley wears a light gray sweater with green Christmas trees, a pale scarf around her neck, a cute wool cap with a tassel, and mittens. She looks pretty. For a moment Ruth is self-conscious of her brown corduroy coat a couple years old, the sleeves tugged down over her bare hands for warmth.

Shirley smiles at Ruth. "I missed you," she says.

"Was it fun?"

"Promise you'll come next year?"

"I will!"

They grin at each other.

Ruth points to the rink. "Skate first, then hot chocolate. I want to hear all about Mammoth, everything."

"I know! But let's skate another time? My legs are so sore from skiing. God, I could hardly make it up the steps!" She rubs her legs, looking at Ruth. "Is that okay?"

"Sure, if your legs are sore…"

"We can still have hot chocolate and talk?"

Ruth smiles. "It's fine!"

"Shall we get hot chocolate? It's at the other end of the rink." Shirley studies Ruth's face.

"I don't feel like wading through everybody," Ruth says.

"I'll go!"

"But your legs are sore."

"Are you mad?"

"No!"

"I can skate. Just need to warm up my legs." Shirley begins rubbing her thighs.

"No, and to tell you the truth, I didn't want to skate anyway!" Ruth laughs.

"Really?"

"I want to hear about Mammoth. I could tell on the phone it wasn't just skiing."

"You could?"

"You sounded like a cat who caught a mouse," Ruth says.

Music fills the air, they lean close to each other and talk, Shirley gestures with her hands and Ruth listens, her hands pressed together in her lap.

In a lift line on the mountain Shirley found herself next to Molly, a girl from school, and with her were two older boys. That evening they had dinner together in the lodge. One of the boys had a flask and they snuck whisky into their sodas. The boy with the flask was Connor. He walked Shirley back to the cabin later that night.

"It was snowing, little flakes drifting down. It was pretty," Shirley says. "As we walked his arm bumped against mine, so I bumped him back. After a couple of those he held my hand. I thought, 'Hmm, he's holding my hand.'"

Ruth nods.

"Near the cabin but still kind of in the trees, we stopped and he looked at me, and kissed me. It was a nice kiss, exactly at the right time. And that was all. He didn't try to kiss me again or grab me. He wanted to walk me to the door but I told him my parents shouldn't see him. So he said goodbye and walked away, under the light snow, in the moonlight. It was perfect."

"So romantic."

"Yeah. The next night we did it again. And we advanced a little."

"How far?"

"I found out what icy hands on my boobs feels like. Not so good, actually."

"Your bare skin?"

"We were in the trees. No one could see us. The next day, we met at his cabin."

"You went to his cabin?"
"His parents were skiing."
"What did you do?"
"Went inside."
"Then what happened?"
"Talked."
"And then?"
"Everything."
"Everything?"
"Everything."

On the way home Ruth absentmindedly answers her father's questions. She lies and says she skated. Kazu asks more questions, and she lies about them too, staring out the window.

"Virginity is only a matter of inches," Shirley said at the ice rink. In the dark of her bedroom Ruth thinks of how far those inches have taken Shirley. She thinks of what Kazu once told her and Hank, about a temple in Japan where people crawl through a hole cut into a large wooden pillar. The person who crawls in, so they say, is not the same person who crawls out.

Christmas is only a few days away. Ruth finds an origami book. She folds a cat for Hank and a crane for Shirley. It takes her many attempts with each before they meet her satisfaction. She puts them in small boxes and wraps the boxes in Christmas paper she and Hank have hidden in their closet for years.

"It's a shame Mother won't let us celebrate. What's the harm in giving a present?" Kazu says. Ruth can see he enjoys being in on their secret.

On Christmas Eve, when Hank is busy with his chores, Ruth goes to his room and puts the present under his bed. In the dark that night she wonders if Hank has given her anything. She could simply reach under the bed to feel if a gift is there. But years ago they agreed it would be breaking a rule. It was her rule, one she made to keep Hank from cheating, giving a present only if he found one from her. No, she must wait until morning. Then she will see. She is certain nothing is there because Hank barely speaks to her. He stares at her suspiciously, as if she means him harm. She asks about his day and how he is feeling, but he only grunts and says nothing.

In the morning, the first thing she does upon opening her eyes is lean halfway out of bed and peer underneath. There is a small package. Grasping it gives her a feeling of joy. It does not matter what it is. She unwraps the paper where he has written the words, *To Ruth, from Hank. Merry Christmas.* Inside is a small bottle of moisturizing lotion for dry hands.

Chapter Seven

She will go to a cave with others from her church. Though she has never met any members she thinks of them as her brothers and sisters. The cave is in Israel, in a mountain far away in a desert, with rock walls as smooth as marble. Far into the mountain the cave goes, the passageway will take them deep underground. Light comes through small openings from the world above. There is a stream of fresh water and pools. They will have everything that is needed. Manna from Heaven as God sent to Moses.

"God made it for us, and it will be perfect."

They are gathered in the living room, Alice, Kazu, Ruth, and Hank. Alice has spent several months in pain, lying in bed. Now she has risen and asked the family to listen to her plan.

"We can all go. God will protect us."

Kazu keeps his eyes lowered. Ruth and Hank do the same, except when turning to glance at each other.

"It will be the only safe place."

They are silent, contemplating her words.

Alice gazes at them with a look of sadness and love. "I will go alone if I have to."

Kazu grimaces.

"It's okay," Alice says, putting her hand on his arm.

On alternate days from Beverly Hills, Kazu drives his old truck south on Highway 101. He looks forward to his early morning journey along the beaches, the sun rising over an ocean bluer than the sky. Surfers glide in their black wetsuits on the water like seals. Sometimes he pulls off the highway to watch them ride ahead of the crumbling wave. It is beautiful. He cannot imagine how free they must feel.

As he drives he thinks about Alice and her beliefs. The cave, prophecies of doom, the rising of a beast, a chariot flying through the sky with spinning wheels of fire. Even if the cave is real, how will she go all the way to Israel when she can barely get out of bed? Last night she spoke with strange lucidity. She knew the cost of plane tickets, where her church will meet in Florida, and other details about traveling from there to New York, to London, to Spain, to Israel. Information she has never mentioned before. Everything the Bible predicts is coming true, she claimed, falling into place as proof of His plan. It is getting close, a matter of months, not longer than a year.

"I'm really going. If you come, the children will come. We can be together."

"Honey."

"But I'm going. Even if I have to walk, I'm going." Her eyes, crystallized by pain, were hard and clear.

He knows she will not really go. When the time comes he expects a crisis, but it is physically impossible. Over the years he watched pain occupy her body like a spirit she must struggle with, like someone from a Bible story she reads to Ruth and Hank. The drugs put her into a dream shaped by these stories and this is where she lives.

He drives along the Palos Verdes cliffs into the neighborhood where houses with red tile roofs are terraced into hillsides among trees. He follows small winding streets, his truck rattles up a gentle hill, and he turns onto a long, broad driveway. It is just the third time he has been here, the newest house on this route. Large, with brick planters that overflow with bougainvillea. In the morning sun the windows become a wall of golden light.

He enjoys using the push mower on this well-kept flat lawn, the sound of sharp blades whirling and the green smell of grass clippings as they fly into the catcher. He steps back to admire his straight cutting lines, nods to himself, and turns to stare across the ocean, letting himself pause and sigh.

The air is filled with the scents of saltwater and pine. It is a gardening route to covet. Set up a sprinkler, clip a few bushes, wash down the driveway, and onto the next one. Like Beverly Hills, his clients here are wealthy Caucasians who pay on time. They have lovely houses with beautiful swimming pools and concrete patios. Ah, to live in a place like this.

It was Fuzzy Takahashi, a friend from the Army, who convinced Kazu to try gardening. They were soldiers of the 442nd Infantry Regiment, the most decorated in U.S. military history, but it didn't matter. "Criminals," people said. They couldn't get a job. Many had to start their own business. Gardening was a popular one.

"I don't know anything about it," he told Fuzzy, shaking his head.

"It doesn't matter! They think we do."

In the beginning Kazu was terrified. When customers wanted advice about their yards he simply did not know what to say. Out of pure fear he mumbled and fell to rubbing his jaw in silence. Amazingly, it was the perfect thing! He learned that by saying nothing they eventually told him exactly what should be done.

"I want an Oriental look, sort of a tea garden kind of deal, some bamboo, a couple of those midget trees, natural looking boulders, you know what I mean."

"Oh, yes," Kazu nodded, "how about here, and here, and over there," randomly pointing at the first empty spots he saw between bushes.

"Exactly! Beautiful!"

Later, standing with the owner and looking at the dead plants, Kazu could say, "I was afraid of this, you know. Wrong climate. But I thought, 'Hey, what the heck? If it's what you want, let's give it a go!'" This was usually met with a handshake and a clap on the back.

Thinking back on those early days and how far he has come gives him a sense of accomplishment. The work can be difficult and he must be careful not to strain or irritate his colostomy, but it is better than laboring in an office with other people, his colostomy gurgling and stinking without warning. Out here he does not see anybody but the occasional passerby walking a small dog or the owner of the house driving away in an expensive car.

His customers are nice. Wives wave at him through the windows. There is one who likes to say hello. She has silvery blonde hair and is fond of bright orange earrings. She brings him a cup of coffee and a small plate of cookies on his weekly visits, handing him the plate and lifting her palms to the heavens to praise the glorious weather, then returning to the house without giving him time to reply. Which is fine. Kazu is glad not to talk. Too often he hears someone say, "Your English is very good." He tries not to let the compliment bother him. He tells himself it doesn't matter. A small, insignificant quirk of Caucasian people trying to be friendly. What do they know? There is a lot he does not understand about them, as well.

The day passes and he goes from house to house. In the afternoon he drives a mile or so along a small road that hugs the cliff and parks. He gets out of the truck, stretches, and walks to a large flat boulder where he sits a couple hundred feet above the ocean. He lights a cigarette and smokes, contemplating the unending blueness shimmering before him in the sun.

He allows himself one cigarette a week. He gave up smoking years ago, after the war. Alice hated it, and he wanted to impress her, and he threw his last cigarette out the car window and told her he would never smoke again. The look of admiration on her face. And he never did, until a month later. Why not? It is just once a week. It is not really smoking. Is it wrong to allow himself this pleasure? To quit smoking took commitment and discipline, but smoking only once a week, and hiding it successfully from his family, takes even more commitment and discipline.

Especially here where the vast ocean and a cigarette fills him with peace. Kazu cannot do without these moments. If he lost every customer in Palos Verdes he would say nothing and return once a week to sit on this flat rock and smoke. One of the few places his head is quiet.

Except for now, as his thoughts are heavy with worry about Alice. The look on their children's faces as she spoke of leaving them when God comes back to earth. There are two different worlds, Alice in one, he and the children in another. Each world has its own life and nothing from one world makes sense in the other.

He smokes, taps away ash, watches the wind catch and carry it away.

"I didn't know until I was forced to know," she once said. It was after she threw the morphine away and suffered almost a month without it. He still doesn't know what she meant. He doesn't want to ask. Her answers are never clear and often leave him feeling worse than before.

Watching her in pain, he begged her to go back on the morphine, and she did. Less pain, but more dreaming. His hopes used to rise and fall with hers, until without faith he lost hope. Now he watches from a distance as she discovers yet another sign, another spiritual reason for her illness, another indication from the Bible of how she will be cured. He is trapped between her world and his. Neither gives him much to enjoy. He inhales the smoke gratefully.

There is a poker game tonight, a once-a-month event. Ruth will be home to stay with Alice. He wants Ruth to go out for the evening.

All she does is hang around the house and study. She ice skated with Shirley Carson last week. At least there was that. He wants her to experience life, have fun, have hope. The game is not that important, he'd give it up for her. But Ruth insists on staying home. She is so stubborn. So it doesn't matter, he might as well go. At least he can win money.

He worries and wonders if all those years, staying home, taking care of Alice, made Ruth unable to do anything else. Now Hank can take her place and her time is mostly free. Why can't she get out and be like other girls? He doesn't know what other girls do when they get out, but whatever it is must be better than staying home every night by herself. Perhaps if she went to church. Church people have committees that Ruth can join.

She is friends with Shirley Carson. He doesn't know the Carson family well, feels bad for them.

Kazu sighs. He walks back to the truck and finds the pack of cigarettes hidden behind a note pad in the glove box. He shakes one out and returns to the flat rock and sits. He looks at it. Will this be his second one today, or his third? Of course he knows it will be his third. But just this once. He won't do it again. It's just that today there are so many things to worry about. Kazu lights up and tosses the match away.

His children are different. Ruth is so good. She stays home and helps. But Hank…what kind of boy is he? How can he grumble about taking care of his own mother? He doesn't say anything, it is the expression on his face, the way he says "Okay" in a flat voice. It gives Kazu an ache in his stomach just thinking about it. At Hank's age he could drive a tractor, plow fields, split wood, fix things. When money was low they ate what they grew on the farm they leased, which was lettuce. Lettuce fried with eggs for breakfast, lettuce fried with bacon for lunch, lettuce ohitashi for dinner. They told each other they liked it! He and his brother and their five sisters, just kids, all working like adults. Pops was killed in a hit and run, his body left on the road like a dog as he lay dying. They took a day to mourn and bury him, and went back to work. It was all work. Hard work. The move to Chicago, the eight of them crammed into a two-bedroom apartment. Mom in her old coat, a scarf wrapped around her hair, pulling boxes of fish on a sled from the warehouse up the icy street to a stall they rented on West 4th near the port. They worked together, gutting and cleaning fish, taking orders, wrapping fish in newspaper and string, tending to sales of canned goods, candles, and soap. They struggled together as a family. Did they complain or lose themselves in gloom? No! They had *gaman*. They had self-respect. They were proud to help each other. They returned to the west coast in the summer of 1941, settling in Los Angeles just in time for Pearl Harbor, then Executive Order 9066, and then everything else. After the war his sisters and mom went permanently back east, they'd had it with the west coast. Mom died, the sisters married and began families of their own. He never sees them anymore. And yet Hank has but a few chores to do, plenty of food to eat, his very own room, but acts like the weight of the world is on his shoulders. Ah! Kazu shakes his head. He doesn't like to compare the two children, one good, the other bad. But he's never had to tell Ruth how to act. She just knows. She does things right. Hank does not.

Disciple and hard work. Responsibility and dedication. Loyalty. Humility, the thinking of others before oneself. These things are nothing special, they are ordinary for human beings and shouldn't have to be explained. If Hank would just open his eyes and look around. He says he wants a life. Well, he has a life!

His friends tell him not to worry about Hank. Each generation is weaker than the one before. But his son is different than even others his age. How can that be? He and Hank share blood. There must be something left!

He takes a last drag and exhales thoughtfully. Perhaps Hank has a mental affliction, what they call *psychological*. Kazu sighs, tosses his cigarette off the cliff as though disposing of evidence, and returns to work.

The game is at Hash Hashimoto's house with Army buddies from the 442. They play a mishmash of five card draw, gin rummy, and Old Maid, a game they learned from the Hawaii boys of the 100th battalion. They played it overseas in France with airplane spotter cards—army-issued poker decks with photos of enemy planes for identification—betting with cigarettes, matchsticks, or small rocks. Tonight they play with nickels, dimes and quarters. They drink whiskey and beer, and smoke, and the kitchen air is hazy. They've been playing for five hours. Their voices rise and fall with laughter and endearing insults.

"Aw, you son-of-a-bitch."

"You dirty dog."

Bess, Hash's wife, does not like being around for card games. She would rather rotate houses each month. But the other wives do not mind the card games and they hang around, even coming into the room occasionally to watch, and the men cannot cuss or drink as much as they like. Bess always leaves on poker nights—"So much drinking, so noisy!"—so the men like to come here where they can be themselves.

Kazu bets a nickel and leans back in the chair to adjust his pants for the third or fourth time. He loosened his belt when he first sat down. Something about the new seal on the colostomy bag isn't right.

Hash calls Kazu's nickel and raises a quarter.

Eto Tanaka's round shoulders slump forward as though from the weight of his large head. His small eyes move constantly around the kitchen as they play cards. "Hash, when you gonna fix the sink? Pride of ownership, eh?"

Hash scratches at his eyebrow, and then, a moment later, his crewcut. He stares at Eto. "In or out?" Kazu watches him, knowing Hash gets itchy when he bluffs.

Eto smokes a cigar. His black hair is thinning. He throws his cards down in disgust.

"This game. Stupid game. Where did we learn this game?"

"Shelby," Melon Watanabe says, waving away smoke from Eto's cigar. Before the war he was known as Watermelon Watanabe, then just Melon, because his family grew them on their farm. People that don't know him from before think his name is Melon because of his bald head.

"From a Buddhahead in the 100th."

"Shimizu."

"Had cousins on the mainland."

"I knew them from San Anita. A guy and his sister. Nice-looking sister," Melon says, pushing a nickel into the pot.

Kazu raises fifteen cents. Everyone folds. Kazu wins with nothing. He holds back a smile as he gathers the coins and stacks them.

"She married a fella at camp."

"Howard Sato."

"Tim. Timmy Sato."

"That was him."

"K-I-A. Vosges."

The men are quiet for a moment, thinking about Vosges.

"That guy didn't blink."

"Pass the bottle."

"They had a kid."

"Never got to see his kid."

"I'll take one."

"She remarried. Moved to Sacramento."

"I hear she's still good-looking."

"Kaz, your deal."

Kazu shuffles the deck. His colostomy gurgles loudly. The men ignore it, just as they ignore how he fidgets to adjust his pants or loosen his belt.

Eto glances at his cards. "Ruth, honor roll at school? That's the word," he says.

"She's doing okay," Kazu says.

"If she's so smart, how can she be your daughter?"

Everyone laughs at the obvious set-up. Kazu sees the Old Maid in his hand, which the rules for tonight say he has to keep. Now an odor drifts up from his pants. Damn seal. Irritates his skin raw yet doesn't do its job. He decides to say something so the men don't have to pretend not to notice. "It's acting up tonight!" He grins and shakes his head. His friends chuckle. Hash bets a nickel and everyone stays in. Eto asks for three cards.

A skinny old man wearing gray pajamas and worn flip-flops shuffles into the kitchen. His white hair is uncombed, his face unshaven. Age spots from the sun float on his skin like small islands. He barely glances at the men, only thrusts his lower lip out in acknowledgement.

"Hey, Pops!" Hash says. "Did we wake you?"

"*Hashimoto-san. Genki desu ka?*" the men shout. Without looking at them, he lifts his hand. Kazu wondered when he would appear.

He finds a stool in the corner and sits, yawns, rubs his hands together as if trying to warm them. Hash brings him a bottle of beer. He shakes his head and points. Hash puts the beer bottle down and pours whisky into a glass. The old man nods and takes a sip. He inhales sharply through his nose, his nostrils flaring. "Ahh…" he says, and smiles. His eyes crinkle happily. Hash lights a cigarette and gives it to him. The old man puffs away, closes his eyes, exhales.

Bess doesn't let her father-in-law drink or smoke, she says it's unhealthy for him, and so he drinks and smokes when she is not there. Kazu wonders if someday it will be like that for him, his kids telling him what to do. He hopes Ruth will be like Hash and sneak him drinks and cigarettes. Hank, he's not sure about. Hank might keep the whisky all for himself.

"Who made the macaroni salad?"

"Joe's wife."

"Your wife? It's different than usual."

"She put in pineapple chunks."

"Try some, Pops." Hash gives his father a bowl and a spoon. The old man tastes it, nods, and mumbles, "*Oishi*."

"Running low on senbei here," someone says.

Hash gets the bag of rice crackers and refills the bowl. He offers the bowl first to his father. The old man takes a handful and sprinkles it on his macaroni salad.

He watches them play cards for a while, then returns to his room. Everybody wishes him goodnight.

"He looks strong," Kazu says.

"Issei are tough."

"Yeah…but his mind…he keeps telling me about the discount he got on Mom's grave ten years ago."

"He got a discount?"

"A hundred bucks off, new customer. He keeps telling me like I don't know."

"Tell about the rat trap," Kazu says.

"Our backyard had this part was overgrown with brush where a bunch of rats lived. Brown rats, rough-looking bastards. Big. They were always there, creeping around. I don't know if they were in the ground or whatnot. He built a tent frame with sticks over where they lived and covered it with plastic. Then he caught a couple feral cats and shut them up inside and sealed off every opening."

"How'd he catch the cats?"

"Oh, you know. A fish head, a big box, a stick. He tied a string to the stick and hid behind some bushes. He had to wait a long time. But he had a bottle to wait with."

They all laugh.

"He punched air holes in the top of the tent and left it like that. After a week or two weeks, I can't remember, he cut a hole in the side. We saw a cat's head come out, look around, then the cat jumped out and ran away, and the other cat came after it. They were fatter than before, got some good rat meat."

The men laugh.

"He took everything down, cleared the brushes away and planted a garden. My dad was clever."

"That generation knew how to do things."

"It wasn't easy for them."

"Whose deal?"

Kazu shuffles and flicks out the cards.

Eto sips his whisky looking at his hand.

"Kaz," he says, "I saw your boy. His hair's long. I thought it was a girl."

Kazu deals himself two cards and ignores Eto. He knows Eto is trying to rile him up and throw off his game. Kazu is winning and much of it from Eto, who plays like a kid. He glances at his cards. Another queen.

"He's a knucklehead," Kazu laughs.

"Like his old man," Hash says.

"Give him a haircut," Eto says.

Melon rubs his bald head. "Damnit. If I could grow long hair, I would!"

"If you could grow any hair."

"If he could grow hair, a golf ball could grow hair."

The men laugh.

Eto stares at Melon without smiling. "A golf ball has more brains."

Kazu remembers meeting Eto in camp. He was a quiet and thoughtful man. Everyone liked him. When they shipped out Eto got his head rattled. Now no one likes him as much as they did before.

They finish the hand. Kazu wins on the pair of queens.

"Ante up, you bastards."

It is Eto's turn to deal and he fumbles with the cards.

"Jesus, he's all thumbs."

"He's doing it on purpose."

"You notice when he deals, he wins?"

"*Sansei*," Eto says in a gruff voice. "Some of them could do better."

Eto believes that Hank makes them look bad in front of hakujin. Why do they still care about what hakujin think? But they do. Eto won't say it out loud because the other men will find it ill-mannered. But Kazu knows what he thinks.

"They try," Kazu says. "Who knows what they can do when chips are down? Damn belt line," he mutters, adjusting his pants.

"Different generation," Joe Yamada says, sitting next to Eto. Joe is a tall man with a dull-looking face. He pulled Eto to safety under fire.

"Who knew what we could do?" Melon says, and raises his glass.

Eto gazes at them.

Hash sweeps the pile of coins to himself, laughing. It is his turn to deal.

"Jeez Louise. Just one. It's all I need," Melon says. When it's his time to bet he raises twenty cents.

Kazu sighs and looks disappointed.

Hash pushes three dimes into the pot.

Kazu wins on the straight he was building.

"Lady Luck. Where are you?"

"With handsome men like me."

Eto puffs on his cigar and motions for the bottle of whiskey. He's been losing all night. He watches as Joe refills his glass, gulps it down, and motions for Joe to pour again.

"I saw Yuki Nakamura on the street the other day, by Little Tokyo," Eto says, wiping his mouth with the back of his hand.

"Nakamura. Has that kid, Tak? The one got a pencil in his eye?"

"What a bum," Eto says. "No real job. Sweeps storefronts, washes windows. A bum."

"Well, I don't know about that."

"He's a good guy."

"Spends a lot of time at the Peppermint Lounge," Joe says.

"A bum," says Eto, his voice loud.

"He had a hard time in camp."

"Just him?" Eto says.

"He was an artist," Hash says. "A pretty good one. You see the poster for O-Bon?"

"He's got talent," says Kazu.

Eto puffs on his cigar and looks at Hash. "An artist? So he's queer, too."

Kazu shrugs, taps his finger on the cards he was going to shuffle. Then deals. They play a few more hands but the joking has died down.

Melon clears his throat.

Hash stands and pours the dregs of his beer into the sink.

Melon looks at his wristwatch, stretches his arms above his head, yawns.

Joe counts his stack of coins.

"Bess will be home early," says Hash. "Let's pack it up."

Kazu is already scooping his winnings into a small cloth bag.

The men clean the kitchen and open the windows to air out the smoke. Afterwards, Kazu and Hash stand on the quiet, dark street.

"Joe said Eto's been drinking a lot. Seems to be true," Hash says.

"That's good for brain injury."
"He really is kotonk."
"But not from a coconut or buddhahead."
"From the Panzer came over that hill."
"I almost feel bad about taking his money."
"I can see it is painful."
"Tell Bess thanks for us."
"I will."
"All right. Well, goodnight."

"You know what this is?" Tak says.
"A cigarette."
"A joint. Marijuana. Your dad home?"
"Nah, he's got poker night. Let's go to the shed."
They walk into Hank's back yard, where the shed is behind the garbage cans. Tall eucalyptus trees act like a fence between their property and the house of a Mexican family, a mom and dad and four children that Hank and Ruth wave to when they see them. Two of the children are outside now, watching. Hank sees them but doesn't wave.

All extra junk from the house goes into the shed. Hank sees boxes and old lamps they moved out from his room and put here. Among other things are a hundred or so bowling pins Kazu rescued from a bowling alley that was being torn down. He never said why he wanted them. The white wooden pins with red zigzag lines are stacked neatly like bottles of wine in a cellar. There is also a broken gas lawnmower on top of an old mattress, and a coiled water hose Kazu found on the road one day and put in the back of his truck. He discovered the hose leaked but he didn't want to throw it away.

They sit on the mattress.
"Where'd you get it?"
"A vato in our apartment building. He got cousins in TJ."

"What does it do?"

"Makes you laugh. Try to hold it in your lungs."

Hank tries, but he coughs out the smoke.

"Hehe, try again."

They smoke it down to the end. Tak takes a small clip from his pocket.

"See this? It's a roach clip. You know why it's called that?"

"No."

"Because this is a roach." Tak holds up the small end of the joint, a bright ember still glowing at the end.

"Shit." It drops from his fingers. He gropes for it, patting the mattress.

"Ah, fuck it."

They sit in the semi-darkness. Hank isn't sure if he feels any different.

"Look at those fucking bowling pins."

Hank thinks about Kazu bringing the pins home, taking the time to make a neat stack, then forgetting about them.

"What was your dad going to do? Start a bowling alley?"

Hank begins laughing. It is the funniest thing he has ever heard. They both start laughing and can't stop.

"A bowling alley!"

"He's going to make a bowling alley!"

After Tak leaves Hank goes back to his room but there is nothing to do. He finds that he is hungry and goes into the kitchen to get something to eat. At first he didn't like how his new room is a little further away from the kitchen. But it's really not. From his room he goes right onto the patio and in just a few steps there is the outside kitchen door. A bowl of potato salad covered with aluminum foil is in the fridge. He crumbles the foil into a ball and tosses it on the counter, eats the potato salad and leaves the bowl and spoon in the sink. He will clean them in the morning. He falls asleep easily that night. Sometime later there is a pounding on his door. It is Ruth.

"Hank, there's a fire!"

"What?"

He dresses and runs outside. The shed is engulfed with a roaring fire that leaps onto the eucalyptus trees. The Mexican family stands in a single line outside their house, the father at one end and descending in height to the smallest boy at the other, their eyes reflecting the bright, swirling flames. A fire truck races into the backyard with lights flashing. Firemen jump down and pull hoses from the truck to squirt the trees until they are no longer burning. The shed drifts to the side and falls down in a small explosion of embers and more flames. "What was in the shed?" he hears one of the firemen ask Kazu.

"Bowling pins."

"Bowling pins?"

"Bowling pins."

Hank returns to his room, thinking about what he and Tak have done. He remembers Tak dropping the roach on the mattress. There was a gas mower on the mattress.

Again, there is knocking on his door. This time it is Kazu. He stands in the doorway, his eyes full of accusation.

"You know anything about it?"

Hank is silent.

"If you know anything, you better tell me."

Ruth is behind Kazu in the darkness of the patio. She peers around their father, looking at Hank with a worried expression.

"No. Yeah."

"What?"

"It was the Mexicans."

"The Mexicans? Why would they do that?"

"I think the kids were playing with matches."

"Did you see them?"

"I think so."

Kazu studies Hank. He sighs, presses his lips together in a tight line, and turns away.

Ruth comes forward, staring at Hank where he sits on the bed.

"Hank."

"What?"

He gives her such a look that she, too, leaves him alone.

Chapter Eight

THE MORNING after vacation the hallways of Venice High are noisy with students returning to school after two weeks of freedom. Their excitement to see each other contrasts with the old school itself: dim hallways, cracked windows, dented gray lockers, classroom doors with graffiti carved into the wood. The vice principal and teachers stalk the campus alert for any sign of joy, for that can only mean students are doing something they should not. Teachers have homework ready to assign as though in revenge. By the end of the day the school will win and send students home like collapsed balloons.

Ruth keeps her eyes straight ahead, not searching for anyone, but enjoying the shouting and laughter in the hallways. It makes her happy to be back in school and she thinks about seeing Shirley at lunch. It's been a few days since the ice rink. She crosses the parking lot where the bus unloads, walks quickly through the outdoor lunch area where tables and benches are chained to the ground, to the banana tree where she turns and climbs the stairway to her locker, then to her first class of the day, Social Studies. It is Mr. Mendez, the same teacher Shirley has for third period.

Ruth and Shirley normally do not see each other in the halls and Ruth has considered going a different way so they can meet. She envies students who pass friends and cheer each other on. She imagines waving to Shirley, shouting, "Hey!" and even, "See you at lunch!" She imagines how their voices will mingle with other hallway voices so students can hear and know that she, too, has a friend. And her friend is Shirley Carson, a pretty girl, popular with upper grade boys. Yes, she is Shirley's close friend, and knows intimacies of her life others can only wonder about. But the routes she takes to her classes are the fastest and she likes to be the first one there. There are parts of school she has never seen because they are outside of where she lets herself roam.

Mr. Mendez is writing on the chalkboard and turns when she enters the room. He greets her with, "Good morning! Welcome back!" He is a handsome, energetic man with black, neatly combed hair. His blue suits, always crisp and orderly. She walks past and recognizes his aftershave, Old Spice, that Kazu sometimes wears. She takes her seat in the front row by the window. From here it is easy to ignore students behind her and their inappropriate chattering as Mr. Mendez tries to teach, their whispered jokes and giggles, the note passing and gossiping about things having nothing to do with the subject of social studies. Sitting by the window she enjoys how the morning light falls partway across her desk in patterns that she notices change throughout the year.

The bell rings. "Good morning! Welcome back!" Mr. Mendez says. "Let's hear from someone about their vacation."

Hands shoot up.

"I went to Mexico."

"*Que bueno!* Did you have a good time?"

"Yes. We stayed on the beach. I drank a margarita."

"My goodness!"

"We went to Hawaii. I went surfing at Waikiki."

"That sounds like so much fun."

"Yes, Charlie. And where did you go?"

"I vacationed at the TG&Y."

The class laughs.

"What did you do, Mr. Mendez?"

"I went skiing at Mammoth. Look," he says, taking off his glasses to show his ski-goggle tan.

"He looks like a raccoon," someone shouts.

"Tell us something that happened."

He puts his finger to his chin and looks upwards as if he hasn't already thought of what to say.

"Hmm, let's see. Well, I was there two days by myself, and then my wife joined me. She's a novice skier and fell down coming off a lift that was moving very fast, and skiers behind piled on top of her, and the operator had to stop the lift. She was so embarrassed."

He embellishes the story with descriptions of bodies flying through the air and rolling down the mountain. The class laughs more and more. He waves his hand and Ruth sees his wedding band, remembering what Shirley said about him and Miss Parker. Is it possible? That he can stand before the class and tell a story about his wife? Yet, here he is doing so.

She has liked Mr. Mendez, but now she thinks of him as a liar, telling a funny story about his wife as though everything is perfectly normal. Making the class think of him in a way that is not really him. Now he is good, now he is the teacher everyone likes. Now he is making the class laugh. But there is another him, a secret person who does bad, wrong things.

He begins a lesson by writing *1776* on the chalkboard. He underlines it with a flourish. Ruth has a strange thought. She imagines that someday he will meet his other self, the one nobody sees. Perhaps they come upon each other in the hallway of the school building, or even his own house, and are forced to stand face to face. What will he say then?

With her finger she traces the outlines of a shadow on her desk. Who could she share her idea with?

Hank would scoff at her strange, weird thought. Kazu would listen patiently, not understanding what she means at all. Alice would take the moment to say something about God. And what would Shirley say, who has a secret life? As for herself, she doesn't know what to think. She does not have a secret life, there is not another her that does anything surprising.

The bell rings. Mr. Mendez stops her as she is leaving.

"Ruth, did you have a nice vacation?"

"Yes."

"Very good." His kind brown eyes study her with an expression not unlike Dr. Kiyonaga, assessing her, checking to make sure she is all right. Then he turns away to talk and laugh with another student.

In the hallway are loud voices, shouting, someone punching a locker. The thrill of being back in school is gone. She walks quickly, hunching slightly.

Second period is Science. Mrs. Jackson has short brown hair cut close to her head like a man. She stands in front of the class with her hands on her hips.

"Did everyone have a nice vacation?"

"We already heard about everyone's vacation."

"Well, I'm sure there's someone who didn't get a chance to tell about theirs."

"What did you do, Mrs. Jackson?"

"Yeah, we want to hear about you. Did you go anywhere, Mrs. Jackson?"

"I stayed home, read a book, did a little yard work."

"What book did you read?"

"Does your husband help you with yard work?"

"What did he give you for Christmas?"

Mrs. Jackson smiles.

"I know what you're up to. But I'm not one of those teachers who likes to waste time talking about themselves."

"Mrs. Jackson, do you feel that vacations are good for our mental health?"

"Over vacation I made a seating chart."

The class groans.

"Everybody line up against the wall and I will call your names and point to your new seat."

"Why do we have to have a seating chart?" someone whines.

The class grumbles and stands by the walls.

Ruth has top grades in class, Mrs. Jackson calls on her for answers no one else knows, and she expects to keep her front row seat at the two-person desk she shares with Jane, another A student. But Mrs. Jackson calls "Ruth" and points to a desk in the very back. Then she calls "John" and directs the boy to sit with her. Ruth looks at Mrs. Jackson for a moment and their eyes meet. Ruth and John sit down and ignore each other. She recognizes him from math, but they have never spoken.

"Everybody...introduce who you are and tell one interesting thing about yourself."

There is further groaning. Always wanting to obey her teachers, Ruth turns to face the boy.

"My name is Ruth."

"I'm John."

He is skinny, almost scrawny, with dark hair and milky blue eyes. There is a dark mole on his chin. She is taller than him. "We're supposed to say something interesting about ourselves," he says.

Ruth thinks.

"I like to ice skate."

John nods. His chin is thin and longish. He rubs it.

"In summertime my dad takes me to Alaska and we capture penguins for zoos and circuses."

"That's interesting," Ruth says.

John looks pleased.

"Except penguins don't live in Alaska. Only Antarctica," Ruth says. John chuckles and points his finger at her.

When the bell rings she walks past Mrs. Jackson, keeping her eyes straight ahead.

"Ruth, please wait."

Ruth turns, crosses her arms and stands near the chalkboard.

"Ruth, I have a reason for where I seated you."

"Okay."

"Are you mad?"

"No."

"I can see that you are, and I'm sorry, but I need a favor."

Ruth sighs and worries she'll be late for her next class.

"This is between you and me, okay?"

Ruth nods, closing her eyes.

"John is intelligent, but has problems. His mother wants him in the last row because anywhere else makes him nervous. He thinks other students are staring at the back of his head."

"I don't see why I have to sit with him."

"Ruth, your influence will help him do better. I'll give you extra credit."

Ruth does not need extra credit. Still, Mrs. Jackson is famous for never giving extra credit. It would be foolish not to agree.

"Okay."

"Thank you, Ruth."

Physical Education is next, and after that she will spend lunch with Shirley. She changes into her gym clothes and walks lightly to the track. The sky is overcast and cool, she begins to jog slowly until halfway around the track, and then she speeds up. She passes other students walking in small groups. She likes to run. She is good at it and runs smoothly. She loves how it makes her feel, a detached head floating in space. Her thoughts no longer jumble and crowd each other, but stretch before her one thought at a time, like a highway to travel along.

Students who opt out of PE sit in the bleachers smoking. They watch Ruth as she runs by under the gray sky.

Girls she has known for years are also on the track. They smile or wave, but no one runs alongside or invites her to join them. She knows what they think of her, that she is stuck up and feels superior. It is not fair, she thinks, having a secret life that exists only in the minds of others.

Ruth showers quickly, wrapping a towel around herself and dressing underneath. The bell rings, signaling lunch. Finally, she will meet Shirley at their bench. As she walks she gathers her thoughts so as not to waste time. They have only thirty minutes. She wants to hear more about Connor. Did he call? What did he say? What did Shirley say in return?

The outdoor lunch area is already filled with the voices of hundreds of chattering students. She passes through to the apple machine where she puts in coins for two green apples. They roll down and she places them in her bag. She follows the cement path that leads to the bench near the ceramic room where Miss Parker teaches. Shirley is there already, sitting with another girl.

"Ruth!" Shirley calls, waving.

The other girl is blonde and pretty, wearing an expensive jacket over a nice blouse. She looks at Ruth with an upturned, smiling face.

"This is Molly."

"Hi."

"Hi!"

"Molly and I have third period."

"Mr. Mendez," Molly says.

"So," Shirley smiles, "we came out together."

Ruth nods, holding her schoolbooks in front of her.

"She has Mendez for first," Shirley tells Molly.

"Did he tell about his wife falling on the ski lift?" Molly says.

"Yes."

Shirley and Molly look at each other. "Same story," they utter in unison and laugh.

"He pretended he just thought of it," Shirley says.

"I like him, though," Molly says, quickly. "Let's start a fan club!"

Molly slides over to make room for Ruth between her and Shirley. The cement bench, usually cold, is warm from Molly.

A teacher approaches on the cement path.

"Hi, Miss Parker!" Molly calls out.

"Hello, girls. Nice vacation?" Miss Parker has sandy-colored hair in a thick braid. There is clay dust on her shoes.

They answer in one voice, "Yes!"

"Well, I'm off to lunch. Bye, girls."

"Bye, Miss Parker!" They watch as she walks away.

"There she goes, to who knows where?"

"And to who knows who?"

Shirley and Molly giggle, leaning forward to see each other past Ruth.

Ruth says, "Did you see Mr. Mendez at Mammoth?"

"I didn't but…"

"I did," Molly says. "And also," she glances in the direction Miss Parker has gone, "Miss Parker."

Shirley already seems to know this.

"Was she skiing?" Ruth says.

"If you want to call it that."

Molly and Shirley laugh. Ruth draws back a little so they can see each other better.

Molly rocks back and forth, glancing at Ruth and Shirley.

Ruth looks at her wristwatch. "I have to go. I'm supposed to talk to Mrs. Jackson about something."

"What?" Shirley says.

"About extra credit."

"Mrs. Jackson doesn't give extra credit," Molly says.

"That's why I need to talk with her."

They laugh. Ruth stands up. "Nice to meet you," she says to Molly. "Bye," she tells Shirley.

"See ya!" Shirley says, smiling and waving.

Ruth goes a little way and turns around to look back. Molly has moved close to Shirley and they are talking, their heads inclined toward each other. Ruth spends the rest of lunch in the hallway by her locker.

Later, at home in her bedroom, she finds the two apples in her bag. She goes to the kitchen and puts them in the refrigerator. Hank is there and when she leaves he takes one and eats it.

Ruth tells herself it is nothing. They know each other from class, ran into each other at Mammoth, Connor is a friend of Molly's. Naturally, they want to talk. Molly, she imagines, followed Shirley from the classroom at lunch. What could Shirley do?

But on Tuesday, Ruth sees Shirley and Molly again sitting together on the bench. She turns away before they notice her. "Molly has a message for Shirley from Connor," she tells herself.

On Wednesday the bench is empty. She wanders over and sits in the hopes that Shirley will appear, or even both of them. Boys that normally stop to visit pass by. Some wave at her, but others give her a glance and keep walking. How silly she feels sitting alone for all to see. After school she goes to study group hoping to find Shirley there, but she is not. Ruth sits at an empty table and opens a book. She imagines Shirley rushing in late, anxious to talk to her and apologize about Molly. Ruth will laugh and wave her hand like it is nothing. But Ruth spends the study hour with her books open, unable to concentrate. She reads a passage, then realizes she doesn't know what she just read. She rereads the same passage, same result. Her mind drifts. She goes home no less distracted, staring at the ground as she walks.

She is undecided on Thursday about whether to go to their bench or not, but walking from P.E. she sees Shirley and Molly in the parking lot, talking to boys. They are some distance away and Ruth quickly moves out of sight. She keeps walking, not wanting to stand in one place like someone lost.

Miss Parker is coming up the path from the opposite direction. They both smile but say nothing. She wonders if Miss Parker will see Shirley in the parking lot with Molly.

Ruth walks, unsure of what to do, past the bungalows where her math class meets, then along the fence line of the empty baseball field. Leaving that behind she finds herself in a deserted part of the school where she has never been. She follows a faint line of bare earth in the lawn, passing through tall bushes that suddenly open onto an area the size of a room. There is a bench, an old birdbath without water, and a willow tree bare of leaves. Lying on the ground are stone columns as if they had fallen over or are in the process of some kind of construction. Trees grow around to form an enclosure. She hears student voices from the lunch area, but only faintly. She sits on the bench, grateful to have a place to be alone and to think. Unless one follows the trail through the bushes she cannot be seen.

If she could be seen she would appear as a statue, sitting motionless on the bench, not even breathing. But her thoughts are active. A stream of thoughts about Shirley. She wonders why Shirley chose her as a friend. Molly makes sense. Molly is pretty and outgoing, not smart, but fun. In comparison she is not pretty, a good student, a rule follower, a girl without surprises, a boring person who says what is expected, nothing else. She has wondered before what Shirley sees in her. Perhaps Shirley wanted help with school work, but she never asks for help. Besides, Shirley is very smart herself. Ruth isn't sure, she would rather there aren't any reasons. She takes an apple out of her bag, looks at it, puts it back, recalls seeing Shirley and Molly in the parking lot. Shirley leaning forward, having said something funny that made Molly throw her head back and laugh.

She feels sorry for herself. Another thought comes to mind, one that has nagged at her. Why did she want Shirley as a friend? For this too she would rather there isn't a reason, but she knows there is. It feels good to be the friend of someone attractive, someone funny and full of life, as if being Shirley's friend means Ruth is the same. So she has a reason herself, a selfish one.

Sitting, watching trees branches shift in the breeze, she sighs, thinking of the conversations Shirley and Molly will have about boys, for which she has nothing to say.

On weekend mornings, Hank leaves the house to wander through the city. If Tak is in town they meet and wander together. If not, he goes alone. Anything is better than staying home with Ruth. Every day she becomes more like their father. Uptight and tense. What is wrong with her? When she asks, "Do you like school? Are you studying hard?" she has such a desperate expression that Hank wants to punch her in the face.

Hank can tell from the willow tree in their front yard that it is spring, the pale green buds emerging. He learned to tell the seasons from that tree. Spring, summer, fall, winter, the tree looks different. Whether his idea of the seasons corresponds with actual dates or not, he doesn't care. The tree says what season it is, and now the tree says spring.

This morning there was a sprinkle of rain, but now the sky is clear and bright, the air fresh. He walks on, past the pharmacy, the small grocery store, the barber shop, the little takeout food place next to the barber. The barber owns both places and used to run back and forth between them. Every time Hank walks by he remembers having his hair cut when he was a little kid. The time a bell rang next door at the food place and the barber rushed over to fry a hamburger or something. Hank sat in the chair with the sheet tied around his neck and waited for what seemed like an hour.

He stops at the green building that sells animal feed. There is a picture window to look through at a large wooden crate full of hay where a flock of baby chicks run around under a lightbulb. One day he and Tak smoked a joint and stood in front of the window for an hour, watching the chicks dash back and forth. They laughed so hard they fell on the ground. He is supposed to meet Tak here today. As he waits, he looks at the chicks and taps his finger against the glass.

"Hey."

It is Tak, wearing his black leather jacket.

He comes to Hank's side and also taps on the glass. Several chicks gather where they are tapping, twisting their heads to look up at the boys.

"We should a buy a couple, raise them and eat 'em," Tak says.

"Our neighbors had a chicken coop. One day I got inside and chased them. They flew up and crapped on my head."

"Hahaha, fucking chickens."

"I got their eggs and smashed them on the garage." Hank remembers the yellow yolks dripped down the wall. The yolks dried and the stains were there a long time.

"Fucking chickens. I would've killed a couple. Had me some fried chicken."

They turn and walk north in the direction of Washington Boulevard. There is a store that sells mirrors and they look at themselves in the display window as they pass.

A girl approaches on the sidewalk. She wears shorts, slippers, a white blouse. She stares straight ahead as they draw close. Hank stops breathing. He looks to the ground, then again to her. He needs both her and the ground to navigate along the sidewalk. Tak steps behind Hank to let her pass. It is someone Hank recognizes from school. She is Mexican, with long, straight brown hair that shimmers bronze and gold in the sun. Her skin is a color he cannot describe. As she passes her dark eyes flick to his for an instant.

"Did you see that chick?" Tak says.

"Yeah."

"Wow!"

They turn around to look just as she enters the mirror store.

"Come on."

They go back, open the door and step inside. "Leave it to me," Tak says.

Tak strolls about the store, examining mirrors as if considering them for purchase. Hank does not see the girl anywhere. A Mexican lady is behind the counter.

"How much is this mirror?" Tak points to a large mirror in a golden frame that hangs on the wall.

"See the price tag."

Tak inclines his head to look at a small tag on the corner of the frame.

"Hmm," he says loudly. "A very nice mirror."

They walk around the store, but the girl is not there.

"Let's go," Hank whispers.

The woman watches them silently from behind the counter.

"First rate mirrors," says Tak loudly.

"Yes," the woman says.

"Ma'am, did a girl just come in here?" Tak says, approaching the counter.

The woman stares at him.

"That is my daughter. Who are you?"

"Two gentlemen. May we request a word with your daughter?"

"All the boys want a word with my daughter," the woman says in a tired voice.

Behind her a beaded curtain hangs across a doorway to another room. Hank sees a figure standing there in the dark.

"I think it's time for you boys to leave."

On the sidewalk outside, Hank mimics what Tak said. *"May we request a word with your daughter?"*

The boys laugh.

They cross Washington Boulevard and find a bus stop. Tak studies the schedule on the post. "Culver City buses. Worse than Long Beach. Fuck."

They wait. Tak points to a manhole cover in the street. "If you stand on a manhole cover it's illegal for cars to hit you."

"Why don't you stand on it."

"Why don't you."

A rush of traffic comes. They watch cars and trucks speed over the manhole cover.

It is around noon when they get off the bus in Venice. The sun is warm and bright. They come to a liquor store.

"Wait," Tak says.

Behind a trash bin a man with uncombed hair is urinating against the brick wall of the store.

"Sir," Tak says.

The man looks at Tak. A stream of urine appears between his legs and runs down the alleyway.

"Sir, could you buy us a bottle of wine?"

The man gives Tak a look of disgust and turns away.

"You can have some."

The man zips up and wipes his fingers on his pants. "All right."

Tak hands him money and he disappears into the store. He returns and they follow him behind the trash bin where the brick is still wet. The man opens the bag, unscrews the bottle top, and takes a drink. A long drink. Then he takes another long drink. He wipes his arm across his mouth and hands the bag to Tak.

"We'll drink at the beach," Tak says, screwing the cap back on.

"Suit yourself."

The two boys cross the sandy beach and go under the pier. Hank removes his shoes and socks and digs his feet into the soft sand. The rough surface of the greenish water dips in and out of the sun. Small waves crash and wash against the shore. Fishing lines slant down from the pier above. They pass the bottle back and forth.

"Bastard drank almost half."

They finish the bottle. Tak starts to throw it in the water but stops. He tears a piece from the paper bag and finds a pencil in his jacket and writes something.

"What did you write?"

Tak shows it to him. IF YOU ARE READING THIS YOU ARE TRULY FUCKED!

They laugh. Tak puts the note in the bottle and screws down the cap and they climb the stairs to the pier and walk to the very end. Tak throws the bottle as far as he can out into the ocean. An old man and woman wearing wide-brim sun hats watch them in silence. The boys return to under the pier.

"Now what?" Hank says.

Tak finds a joint in his jacket pocket and holds it up.

"*Be prepared*. The Boy Scout motto."

They smoke, watching sea foam rush up the sand to their feet.

"How's your sister?"

"Fine."

"She got a boyfriend?"

"I dunno." It bothers Hank when Tak asks about Ruth.

"You don't talk to her or nothin'?"

"She stuffs toilet paper in her bra. How can I talk to someone like that?"

Hank lies down, stretching out. The wine and marijuana are relaxing and the sand is soft. He closes his eyes and listens to the soft crashing of waves. It is good here, the ocean smells like salt and honey. He thinks about the girl at the mirror store. The most beautiful girl he has ever seen.

Tak is speaking to him, or speaking to himself, Hank is not sure. When Tak smokes he likes to talk, *talk talk talk*. Hank keeps his eyes closed, he knows it doesn't matter if he answers or not. He listens to Tak say he hates living with his mother in Long Beach because she complains all the time.

"I tell her 'Mom, you always say, *Gaman, gaman*, and that Japanese don't complain. But all you do is complain.' I tell her to have gratitude, she's healthy, not like your mom, Hank. Can't get outta bed."

Hank pictures the face of his mother. The same face he always pictures. Her eyes sad and accusing.

"It's my fault," Hank says. It comes out of his mouth before he thinks about it.

"What?"

"That my mom's sick."

"Your fault? How come? She caught it from you?"

Tak moves away from him.

"It's not contagious." Hank opens his eyes and stares at the underside of the pier.

"How is it your fault?"

"Because I made her sick when I was born."

"How do you know?"

"My dad told me."

"What did he say?"

"He said, 'You being born made mom sick.'"

"He said that? When?"

Hank thinks. It is hard for him to remember parts of his childhood. Everything in the past is a blur.

"Elementary school."

"He tell you that again?"

"No. I think he forgot."

"Damn. That make you feel bad?"

"Can't remember. I guess."

"You still feel bad?"

"I don't know. No."

Hank sits up. He sees something bobbing in the water near the shore. "Look." He points.

"Haha, it's our bottle. Let's pretend we're stranded on a desert island and we see the bottle. Look! A bottle. We're saved!" Tak rolls up his pants legs and wades into the water. He brings it excitedly back to Hank.

"There's a note inside! I wonder what it says? You read it."

Hank unscrews the top and shakes out the piece of brown paper. He unfolds it and reads aloud the words he already knows Tak has written: "If you are reading this you are truly fucked!" He lets the strip of paper fall from his hands.

"We're fucked!"

"We're fucked!"

In a sudden burst of energy they leap up and down on the sand, laughing. Tak seizes the bottle and hurls it against one of the cement pilings. It shatters. They laugh more.

Hank sees jagged pieces of sharp glass in the sand.

"Let's go," Tak says.

"Someone's going to step on it." Hank kneels and begins picking up pieces of glass. Tak joins him.

They toss the shards of glass into the shallow water. They look around and don't see any more.

"I think we got it all," Tak says.

"What if someone goes wading under the pier?"

The boys stare into the water.

"Fuck it," says Tak. "At least we tried. Hey, you want this?" He bends down and picks up the scrap of paper with the message.

Hank takes it, reads the words silently, and puts it in his pocket.

Chapter Nine

RUTH SPENDS her lunch breaks at the place she found. It is spring semester and the small willow there is budding. She borrowed a bucket from Miss Parker's room and filled the birdbath. Now bluejays, sparrows, flycatchers and robins visit to drink. She tosses crumbs on the ground and watches the birds twitch their heads, flick their tails, and hop down from the bath to peck in the dirt.

At first, the distant sound of students in the lunch area, their faint laughter and murmer of voices rising and falling, made her lonely. Once she imagined footsteps on the other side of the bushes and froze, but it was nothing. Now her loneliness is less than before and she is glad of her solitude. She turns her face to the springtime sun and sighs happily. Trees sway in the slight breeze. She is content to be here alone with her thoughts. At times, those thoughts include Shirley. But as the days pass those thoughts are less and less, especially now with the new interest that she learned from Miss Parker.

Ruth chose ceramics for her elective with the idea to make useful objects. A coffee cup for Kazu, a container for Alice to keep her medication, a pencil holder for Hank. Miss Parker doesn't mind if she stays after school to work on projects, just the two of them in the studio. At first she made simple things, a slab box, a trivet. Because she stays after school nearly every day Ruth advances into using the wheel before other students do.

She tells Miss Parker one day, "I think I have a passion for this."

"There was a man who cut off his little finger because it got in the way of throwing pots. That's passion," Miss Parker says.

Ruth examines her little finger and imagines it as a stump.

"Let me show you something." Miss Parker takes a pack of cigarettes from the pocket of the long apron she wears. The ceramics studio is apart from the main buildings and Miss Parker only smokes after school and only in front of Ruth, as far as Ruth can tell. She notices, during class, how Miss Parker slides her hand into the apron pocket where her cigarettes are, or pats where they are in her pocket with her hand. Miss Parker opens a sketchbook. She has large blue eyes that Ruth notices can stay open a long time without blinking. In the book are drawings of various clay objects, drawn in pencil from different angles.

"How beautiful."

"Not all mine. These are from an exhibit of Navajo pottery. Nice, aren't they?"

Ruth takes the sketchbook and flips through the pages.

"Are these your drawings?"

"Yes. I sketch ideas so I can change and play with them. I draw the work of other people. You should do this. It teaches your brain to think like an artist."

"Is this drawing of your hand?"

"Yes. Do that, too. Add drawings of other things, do whatever."

"I couldn't draw like this."

"Are you sure? Have you tried? I can show you a few tricks."

Ruth stays after school longer than she ever has and practices drawing. Miss Parker looks on, but says little more than, "That's very nice, Ruth."

Later, someone appears in the doorway. It is Mr. Mendez.

"Hey," he says. "Hi, Ruth!"

"Hi, Mr. Mendez."

"Just passing by," he says.

Miss Parker smiles.

"Well, have a nice weekend," he says.

He walks away and Ruth continues to draw.

Miss Parker lights a cigarette and stands in the doorway, smoking.

On another day Miss Parker says, "I don't see you girls at lunch anymore. I thought the bench is your place."

"Not anymore."

"Found a better place?"

"Yes." It is after school. Ruth sits at a small desk, drawing.

"I need a hand."

Ruth helps Miss Parker move a heavy container of wet clay.

"You've been drawing. That's what you like now."

"I keep up with my projects."

"I know you do."

Miss Parker finds a broom and begins sweeping.

"I can do that," Ruth says.

"It's okay. I like sweeping."

Ruth returns to her drawing.

"I see your friend sometimes. What's her name?"

"Shirley."

"Right. I heard about her little brother, a couple of summers ago. So sad."

"Yes."

"You girls still friends?"

"I don't know. No."

"What happened?"

"I guess I don't know."

Miss Parker empties the dustpan into a trash can and puts the broom away. She pats her apron, finds a cigarette, and stands in the doorway.

She half turns to Ruth. "High school seems like a big deal. But believe me, it's not."

"I know."

"Especially high school relationships. Relationships are fickle." She turns away, lights her cigarette, and is silent.

Ruth continues to draw. She is trying to draw her hand. She has attempted it over and over during the past few weeks but cannot get it right.

Miss Parker turns to watch Ruth. When she finishes her cigarette she stubs it out, drops it into the metal trash bin, and comes to stand by Ruth.

"Let me see what you did before."

Ruth shows her, turning each page of the sketchpad, and finally back to the page she is working on. She looks up at Miss Parker.

Miss Parker is studying the latest attempt.

"Well," she smiles.

Ruth goes back to drawing. Miss Parker sits at her desk, leans back in her chair, and rolls a pencil thoughtfully between her fingers.

Ruth hates sitting next to John. He is not obnoxious or rude, but having to sit in the back of the class for his benefit does not seem fair. She is not a teacher and does not know how to help him as Mrs. Jackson wants. Or if he even wants help. When they see each other later in the day, at Math, he acts like he doesn't know her.

Mrs. Jackson procures frogs for the class to dissect. They are alive and she explains they need to be killed by inserting a pair of scissors sideways into their mouths and snipping off the top half of their heads.

"It's painless for the frog," she says, "but I don't like doing it. Is there a volunteer?"

John's hand shoots up so fast it startles Ruth.

"Okay, John. Can you come in before school tomorrow?"

"Yes!"

For the rest of the class period John is animated, working with Ruth to identify and color frog body parts on a diagram. When the bell rings he says, "You can help me snip off their heads tomorrow. If you want?"

It is the first time Ruth has been asked by a boy to do something. "No, thanks."

John shrugs in disappointment.

The next day, they dissect a green-colored frog together and John is interested and excited, more than he has ever been in class. It reminds Ruth of herself, when she and Hank operated on snails to remove their shells, when she dreamt of being a doctor.

She is always the first student to arrive, and John always the last, often rushing in after the bell. But he begins coming early. They talk before the start of class. His blue, milky eyes, at first unable to meet hers, now seek hers out, and he talks excitedly about random topics, gesturing with his hands, brushing back the dark hair that keeps falling across his face.

He is pale, unnaturally so, it seems to her. She is shocked by how blue the veins on his arms are. "I hate all sports and I hate people who play sports," he says.

"What about people who like to run. Do you hate them?"

"Do you like to run?"

"Yes."

"But running's not a sport."

"Track is a sport."

"Are you on the track team?"

"No."

"Case closed," he smiles.

She doesn't like how he thinks he is smarter than her.

At the beginning of the week, as Mrs. Jackson is talking about Galileo, John leans close to Ruth. "You're pretty," he says.

She keeps her eyes forward. She can feel John watching her. She says nothing and he shifts his body away and spends the rest of the class staring at his desk. They don't speak again during class and he leaves without saying anything. He is absent for the next two days from both Science and Math, the two classes they share.

Ruth recalls his words, the sound of his voice, unsure of what to think. What is she supposed to say to him now? If only she could ask Shirley, but she can't. She thinks about John so much it interferes with her studies. But when he returns to class later that week he acts as though he had never said a thing.

The following Monday he rushes in long after the bell has rung, interrupting what Mrs. Jackson is teaching the class about the atom. He stands in the front of the class, waving his hands, breathing through his mouth. "I'm sorry," he says to Mrs. Jackson. "I didn't sleep. I couldn't. I stayed up all night thinking about Vietnam."

Mrs. Jackson listens.

"Tell us what you were thinking, John."

"We're dropping napalm on people. Innocent people."

"Class, do you know what John's talking about?"

A boy raises his hand. "It's a form of chemical warfare."

"We're burning people up," John says. "Women and children."

Mrs. Jackson turns to the class. "It's not my place to be political, but I think what John said is important for us all to know. Thank you, John."

John slides into the seat next to Ruth and puts his head in his hands, groaning softly. He sighs and turns to her. His eyes are crusty. His face looks terrible, as if he has been crying. A vein pulses in his temple.

His hand slides off the desk and she feels the pressure of it on her knee. He half smiles, as if reassuring her of something.

It is for only a few seconds, then she feels his hand lift away and John ignores her for the rest of the class. She tries to pay attention to what Mrs. Jackson is saying about atoms and electrons and orbits, but her voice is a drone of sound and Ruth cannot discern the meanings. When the bell rings she gets quickly to her feet and hurries out the door. For the rest of the day all she can think about is John, the light, warm pressure of his hand on her knee. She does not want to go to Math, where he will be. But she forces herself, arriving early, refusing to turn around to see if he is sitting in his back-row seat. Halfway through class she still does not know if he is in the room.

The teacher, Mr. Cohen, is explaining a proof. He stops and says, "John, please demonstrate on the board what I was just talking about."

The class titters. Mr. Cohen likes doing this, calling on students who aren't paying attention to come up and make fools of themselves in front everybody.

John walks past where Ruth sits in the front row. Mr. Cohen hands him a piece of chalk and steps back. The class is silent, waiting to see what John will do. He stands before the chalkboard and raises his hand as if to write something. His hand hovers in the air for a long moment, then drops back to his side. He turns to look at the class, his eyes rove across all the faces. He stares at Ruth with a pitiful expression. A few students giggle. In silence, John puts the chalk down and returns to his seat.

"Well done, John," Mr. Cohen says.

The next morning in Science, John is quiet and withdrawn. Slumped in his chair, picking at the skin around his fingernails, running his hand through his hair and sighing. Though Ruth had thought about him during the night, she did not plan on doing this, it just happens. Her leg drifts over to touch his with the lightest pressure. For a moment she knows what a mistake she is making, but it is too late.

Like a small, startled animal, John becomes motionless. He and

Ruth stare straight ahead at the chalkboard where Mrs. Jackson is drawing concentric circles. Their legs press to each other for what to Ruth seems minutes. Nothing else happens. Ruth is about to move her leg away, but John slowly lowers his hand under the desk to cup her knee with his palm. In a moment she feels a light squeeze. Then he leans close and begins to say something, but Mrs. Jackson is still talking, and Ruth pulls her knee away. John falls silent and withdraws his hand. After a moment, Ruth lets her leg touch him again. John hesitates, then his hand finds her knee again and he leans towards her, words already whispering from his lips. Ruth pulls her knee away. Again, he withdraws. She can sense his confusion and fear.

It is her knee, she can do with it as she wants, she decides, and now she understands what can be done. She presses against him a third time. When he returns his hand to her knee, he does so silently, and Ruth lets his hand remain. She leans forward to show how fascinated she is by what Mrs. Jackson is saying about inner-shell electrons. With his hand on her knee, John also leans forward as though listening, his mouth slightly agape.

The year passes. John's grades improve. The struggle in class to keep John's hand from sliding upward is not much of a struggle. John tries every day, but the slightest pressure from her hand on top of his to deny him is enough. No one can see what they are doing under their desk in the back of the room.

He wants to spend lunch with her, but Ruth knows she must consider this carefully. Is that what she wants? She has control of him in class. Somewhere else, the secret place she has found where she daydreams and draws in the sketchbook Miss Parker gave her, will John obey? And if they break up? He will know where to find her, able to intrude upon her whenever he wishes. She's heard stories of boyfriends tracking down the former girlfriend, not leaving her alone. She doesn't want to lose the peaceful, isolated spot she has found. Her own place, where she can think and draw and not worry about other people. She lies and tells him she must study during lunch and does not want to be disturbed. He accepts it with disappointment in his eyes.

There is no one to talk to about John. Occasionally she sees Shirley at school, and if unavoidable they wave. Once, she ran into her at the library, and it was impossible not to say something, so they asked each other how they were, what they were doing. It was awkward. Molly watched them from a table. She imagines telling Miss Parker about John, but she is afraid it will get him into trouble. Or worse, Miss Parker might think that she and John are perverted. Are they? Ruth does not know, only that she likes what they do and looks forward to it.

At the end of the semester, Mrs. Jackson asks Ruth to stay for a minute after science class.

"Ruth, may I talk to you about something?"

"Yes."

Ruth calms herself. She has already decided that if Mrs. Jackson discovers what she and John have been doing, she will admit it at once and take the blame. She has a speech already prepared and she now searches for the opening words.

"Ruth, I said I would give you extra credit for helping John, right?"

"Yes."

"You don't need it, but I'm giving it to you anyway."

"Thank you."

"Ruth, there is something else I want to talk about."

"Okay."

"Have you ever considered becoming a teacher?"

"No."

"I'm saying this because you've made John rise. Beyond my expectations."

"Um, yes."

"It's huge, how much he has risen. How did you do it? I'd like to know so I can do the same for other students like John."

"I encouraged him. That's all."

Mrs. Jackson nods in agreement.

"They say encouragement is the most important thing you can give a student. I know this is a tough class. But when students discover that harder is actually better, they learn to love challenges. I'm going to do for others what you did for John."

"I think it works."

"You would be an excellent teacher. Thank you, Ruth."

"Thank you, Mrs. Jackson."

Hank leaves his class to use the restroom, where he spends a while looking at himself in the mirror and combing his hair, then takes a long, roundabout way back and stops at the water fountain and drinks, admiring the colorful mosaic of gum wads students have spit. Now he stands motionless in the outdoor hallway near his classroom, not knowing what to do. In the small courtyard just yards away is the girl he and Tak followed into the mirror store that day.

They are so close he could talk to her without shouting, yet she seems not to notice him. She gazes at something far away in the blue sky. Hank steps back and peers at her from behind a narrow drainpipe. Sunlight bathes where she stands. Thick-petaled flowers release their scents, filling the warm air with perfume. She turns her head and Hank looks away to stare absently into the sky. Then she is at the corner of the building, walking away.

In the days that follow, Hank asks to leave class for the restroom so often that his teacher wonders aloud if he has a medical condition, but Hank does not see the girl in the courtyard again. He searches for her throughout the school, taking alternative hallways during passing periods in hopes of running into her. Scanning the crowds of students, he never sees her face.

A week passes. At the end of sixth period a note is brought to him, a summons from the vice principal, Mr. Nice. Hank hurries to the office at the front entrance of the school as the other students are joyfully free for the day. The front office is a terrible place, with bright fluorescent lights and a silence deeper than the library. The summons has filled him with guilt and a sudden fear that Mr. Nice knows about his weekend trespassing on school grounds. The lady behind the counter gives him a stern look, squinting her eyes and furrowing her brows, and wordlessly points him down the hallway. He knocks on the vice principal's door. A deep voice says, "Come in."

Mr. Nice has a wooden paddle in his drawer with holes drilled in it. To reduce air resistance, it is said, so he can swing it faster onto a boy and increase the sting. Wind whistles through the holes as the paddle comes down, they say. Every boy in school knows about it, and the ones who experience the paddle like to brag about how much it hurt. Mr. Nice is big and Black, with a bald head and dark eyes that always seem on the verge of laughter, but nobody knows what he might be laughing about.

"Tanazaki. Sit down."

Hank does.

Mr. Nice looks at Hank with his bright, almost-laughing eyes. "How are you doing? Are you having a good first year?"

"Yes. Sir."

"How are your parents? Is your mother feeling better? It's a shame, having something like that."

"She feels better, then worse."

"Are you helpful to her and your father?"

"Yes, sir. I can't stay for long today because I need to get home."

"That's good," Mr. Nice says, slowly nodding his large head. "Tell me, how is your sister, Ruth?"

"She's fine."

"She was a credit to this school. I wish all students could be like her. Tell her hi for me."

"I will."

"Well, I'm not going to keep you. Just want to check in and see if you're doing alright."

"I am. Thank you, sir." Hank leans forward and begins to stand.

"You wouldn't know anything about someone sneaking onto school grounds during the weekends? Two boys, actually, and doing stupid things, like putting trash cans up the flagpole, scratching cuss words onto lockers, hanging soiled Kotex on the bulletin board in the lunch area. Do you know anything about that?"

Hank sits down and raises his eyebrows as though in shock to hear what some people will do. He stares earnestly into Mr. Nice's eyes.

"No, sir! I don't!"

"Because you live near school, don't you? Easy walking distance?"

"Yes, sir."

"Uh huh. Just thought you might have seen something. Apparently it's happened several times during the year, and the weekend janitor gave me a description, but he never saw them up close."

"No, sir. Nothing."

"You let me know if you do, okay?"

"I will, sir."

"All right, then. You have a good day." Mr. Nice stands, rising before Hank like a mountain rising, the look in his eyes saying he knows everything there is to know about Hank, and he finds it amusing. He puts out his hand for Hank to shake. It is the largest hand Hank has ever seen. He tries but cannot get his hand around Mr. Nice's palm and can only shake a couple of the fingers.

As he leaves the office, he thinks of Tak. They better not vandalize anymore. Tak will be sad, but that's how it has to be.

Instead of cutting across the school grounds, he decides to go out the front gate and walk the long way home. As he does, he sees a figure in the near distance that brings him to a halt. It is the girl, walking alone.

Hank wants to follow. But he cannot, he has to check on Alice. It is already taking him longer than usual. He walks quickly, turning to look over his shoulder until he can't see her anymore, then continues walking in a fast pace until he is home.

Chapter Ten

THE FOLLOWING day she is there again, walking by herself. Last night Hank thought about Alice, how she naps every afternoon. There is nothing for him but to tiptoe around the house. Being there or not doesn't make a difference, all she does is sleep. He wishes he could stay after school with other students. He wants to join the garden club. But he has a duty to Mom. And now this, the girl walking alone, the opportunity to introduce himself. It won't hurt if he's a little late. He figured it out last night. "Mom won't even know," he tells himself. "I'm just coming home another way." He crosses the street behind the girl. If she sees him he will appear as just another student leaving school after the day is done.

Why is she never with friends? She could be on her way to meet someone now, an older boy from high school who has a car. The thought makes him slow down and consider turning away. He could be her friend. He'd buy her an ice cream cone. Or french fries and a soda from the lunch place by the lawnmower shop. Or a submarine sandwich from Mile Long Subs across the street from the pharmacy. Or take her to the ice rink. Would she like to ice skate? He's never been there but he's heard about it. He heard about the make-out section at the top of the bleachers. He listened to a group of boys talk about it. One of the boys said he got stinky finger from his girlfriend. Hank wondered what the boy meant, and later asked

Ruth. But Ruth only looked at him with large eyes like she does when she is embarrassed, and claimed not to know what he was talking about.

Tak explained it to him. But he does not want that from the girl he is following. French fries and a soda would be good enough.

The afternoon is warm as he follows her, too warm for the jacket he wears. He takes it off and slings it over his shoulder, imagining how he will appear if she looks his way. He thinks of John Wayne. It's how John Wayne would carry a jacket. What if he drapes it over his arm? He does so, again imagining how he looks. It is gentlemanly, the way a scientist would carry a jacket. Or a librarian. He switches it back to his shoulder.

A car rolls by. Voices call out the window at the girl, but she acts as though she does not hear, and the car speeds away, speeding up and braking, speeding up and braking, jumping up and down the street.

Hank quickens his pace and draws closer. Now he is only several feet behind.

Abruptly she stops and turns to face him. They watch each other. She does not say a word, merely looks at him with her dark eyes, her face so beautiful he feels a pain in his stomach. He returns her gaze dumbly.

Her eyes lose interest and she turns away. Hank sighs. He goes in the other direction towards home.

Alice is sleeping as he knew she would be. He makes a peanut butter and jelly sandwich and goes to his room to think about the girl. But there's not much to think about, only how they looked at each other and how he failed to do anything. He was so close to her. He sits on his bed, opens a comic book, and begins reading. He hears Ruth come home. In a little while she knocks on his door.

"Did you see Mom, Hank?"

"She's sleeping."

"She doesn't feel good."

"I know. She never feels good."

"She got up to call Dr. Kiyonaga, but he wasn't there."

Hank turns the pages of his comic book.

"I'll be in the kitchen."

"Leave the door open, it's stuffy in here," Hank says.

Later, he hears Kazu's truck drive into the backyard. Hank thinks about closing the door, but by that time his father is already walking past. In a few minutes Kazu returns.

"How was Mom when you got home?"

"Sleeping."

"She's not feeling so good."

"That's what Ruth said."

Kazu nods.

"I have to go out again. You and Ruth keep an eye on Mom."

"Where are you going?"

"The nursery. Pick up plants."

Hank looks up from his comic book. At school kids were talking about Hotdog Heaven. "Can I have a ride to Washington Place, Dad? Hotdog Heaven has all you can eat for a dollar."

Kazu is silent.

"It's on the way and I'll be waiting on the street when you come back."

Kazu sighs.

"Ruth's here," Hank reminds him.

"Okay. Sure," Kazu says.

Hank finds a dollar and runs after Kazu, helping to unload mowers from the truck to make room for plants. They drive up the dirt road.

"How was work today, Dad?"

"Same as always."

Hank nods and becomes quiet. His father is mad about something.

"Roll up the window, dust is coming in."

Hank rolls up the window of the cab. The truck rattles over a deep rut. He wonders if Kazu knows he didn't come home right away after school. But only Alice could have told him and she didn't know because she was sleeping. It is impossible his father can know. Hank relaxes a little. They turn left onto Centinela Avenue and ride in silence. Hank's thoughts find their way back to the girl. How they stood so close. She was waiting for him to make the first move. He knows it! What would John Wayne do? He'd take the girl in his arms and kiss her until she fainted.

They bump over the train tracks and pass through two blocks of small businesses. No other cars are on the road. He sees that Kazu is driving in the middle of the street, the truck straddling the broken yellow line.

"Dad, you're riding the line."

Kazu swerves back into the lane.

"What did you say?"

"I only said you were riding the line, Dad."

Kazu is silent, staring. There is a moment when Hank knows he has done something wrong, but he does not know what. He said something. He didn't mean anything bad by it. He was trying to be helpful. But now the yelling begins. Not physical blows, his father never strikes him, but the shouting and the words are like blows and Hank wishes they were. Maybe he'd like it better that way. It would hurt at first. But the anger in his father's voice and the words he says stay with Hank forever. His father has said things, years ago, that still hurt to remember even after all this time. Then the strange thing happens that has happened before. Kazu's voice is suddenly quiet, barely discernible, as though someone turned down the volume on a radio. The angry expression on his father's face, the mouth opening and closing, the eyes widening, reminds Hank of a goldfish, exaggerated and comical, like an old movie. Hank feels himself withdrawing far away from what is happening. It is not him but someone else who is being yelled at.

At Washington Place the truck pulls to the curb and Hank gets out. "Thank you for the ride, Dad," he mumbles, closing the door softly, and walks east toward the freeway against traffic. Hotdog Heaven is only a few blocks further on but he has forgotten about it. The late afternoon air is heavy. He sits on a bench at the first bus stop he comes to. A large flatbed rumbles past, black smoke streams from silver exhaust pipes above the cab. Chrome strips around the windows of cars glint in the harsh light.

He was numb, but everything now is raw and close. Traffic rushes just feet away from him, horns blare, the stink of tar rises in waves of heat from black asphalt, a man's giant face on a billboard smokes Lucky Strikes, a jet shrieks overhead. Across the street, cars pull into a gas station where uniformed attendants run to greet them. A thickset woman wearing a dirty pink housecoat, curlers in her hair wrapped with a red scarf, sits at the other end of the bus stop bench. "Balls, balls, balls," she screams. "Fucking balls!"

A bus arrives and Hank boards it. He stares out the window on the way to the beach. At Venice Pier he gets out.

Leaving the boardwalk, carrying his shoes and socks, he crosses the warm sand to the shoreline. An orange sun sits on the horizon. Pink and golden clouds and thick ropes of light fill the sky. Here and there across the beach figures stand quietly like pilgrims. The salty air, the crashing waves. The top of the sun forms a glowing mushroom shape before it disappears.

He sits in the soft sand. People stroll barefoot along the tideline where foaming waters rush over their feet. The wind picks up a little.

The wind blows Hank's hair and he stares across the greying blue sea to the horizon. He clasps his knees and rocks back and forth, or sits motionless, sometimes sighing. He could travel back a million years and everything would look the same as it does now. Or a million years into the future. "The same either way," he thinks.

The light fades and the beach darkens. He returns to the boardwalk and sits on a short brick wall under a streetlamp that crackles with purple light. He brushes sand off his feet and puts on his shoes. He decides to walk home. It is a long way, but he is not in a hurry. There's nothing to do there but go to his small room. Ruth will hear and bring him something to eat as an excuse to talk. It annoys Hank. What does she want from him? She never says anything that matters, and he cannot stand how she hovers. "You're in high school. Find some friends," he wants to say.

He cuts through several neighborhoods. It is Friday night and there are parties. People gather in front yards to barbeque and drink beer. He follows a scattered group of boys and girls his age, and when they turn onto a driveway that goes behind a house he goes with them, remembering how Tak crashed the sports league party. He wonders if he will see anybody from his school.

The back yard is festive with laughter and loud voices. Colored lights hang from wires above, casting a happy glow as music drifts from open windows. He wonders again if he should be here. A group of boys stare at him and he decides the best thing to do is wave. They nod and turn away. He finds a plastic cup and a boy at the keg fills it for him without any questions.

Hank drinks and wanders around the outside of random groups. He drinks and it feels good. He returns to the keg several times and refills his cup.

The back door opens and a man steps out to stand beneath the porch light and gaze around the yard. Hank decides he is the parent. Hank overhears the man saying to a girl nearby, "Are you enjoying yourself?"

"Yes, great party. Thank you!"

"Don't drink too much," the man laughs.

"I won't!"

The man smiles and nods, takes another look around, and disappears inside.

Hank goes to a hedge of tall bushes in the shadows where other boys have been standing. He is urinating when he hears or feels the presence of someone behind. Hank finishes, zips up, and turns around to see two boys waiting for him.

"Hey man, you go to Marina, right?" one of them says. Hank does not recognize him.

"Yeah."

"Hey, all right," the boy says, and offers his hand.

Hank reaches to shake it, but the boy pulls back.

"Didn't wash your hands, man."

The other boy laughs.

"Was you following a girl home today? After school?"

Hank is silent.

"She's here, man. She wants to talk to you."

"She's here?"

"*Ese*, she's here! She wants to talk to you."

"Where is she?" Hank looks around the yard.

"She's over there, by the garage."

"I don't see her."

"She's on the other side, man. She wants to talk to you in secret."

"She don't want no one to know."

"You want to see her or not?"

"Don't be a pussy, man. Go talk to her!"

He remembers what Tak said. A faint heart never won a fair lady.

"Okay."

He walks around the side of the garage, the two boys following. When he turns the corner there are a couple of figures waiting in the dark. He peers into the shadows and sees it is two more boys.

He turns back, but the first two boys block his way.

One of them pokes a finger into Hank's chest.

"Do you, like, always follow girls home? We seen you, man. We drove by."

"You some kind of pervert?"

"No. I'm not."

"You know judo, karate?"

"I did judo when I was little."

"When you were little. So, you don't know it now."

"What about karate?"

"No."

"Do you know how to fight?"

Hank is thinking of what to say when the boy punches him in the stomach. He doubles over and staggers backwards. He can't breathe. Someone catches him and shoves him forward and a fist strikes his face. Then he is grabbed from behind and thrown to the ground. The four boys stand around him in the dark.

"That was my sister, man!" one of them says. The others laugh.

"He's weak."

"Faggot."

Hank lies motionless with his eyes closed, pretending to be unconscious. He listens for sounds, the scraping of their feet to indicate if they are moving closer to him or away, or perhaps some final words they have for him. He hears them leave, waits a minute longer, then gets up and goes back to the street and walks out of the neighborhood.

It is past ten by the time he returns home. The house is quiet, but he does not go inside. He walks around to the patio and unlocks the door to his room.

The punch to his stomach hurt, but as soon as he was able to breathe the pain went away. The punch to his face did not hurt at all. It knocked him backwards but at the time he barely felt it. He touches his jaw, only slightly sore. Getting beat up is not so bad.

Someone knocks on the door. It is Ruth with a look of worry on her face.

"Hank, Mom's in the hospital."

"What?"

Ruth comes inside. "After you and Dad left, Mom rang for me. She wanted to telephone Dr. Kiyonaga, but she couldn't get up, so I called and left a message. When I talked to him, he sent for an ambulance. Dad got here when the ambulance did. I've never seen her like this."

"Where's Dad?"

"He followed her to the hospital. They put an oxygen mask on her. I saw her, she was on a stretcher, they put straps on her. Dad said he'd call."

Hank stares at her.

"It's going to be okay, Hank. I'll let you know when Dad calls." Ruth looks into his eyes. "I'll come back as soon as he calls."

Hank sits on his bed. There have been emergencies before, but this time seems different. "Mom's going to die," he thinks.

A long while passes. What Ruth said comes back to him. "I've never seen her like this."

There is tapping at the door. It's Ruth.

"He hasn't called yet."

They sit together on the bed.

"It's going to be all right, Hank."

She puts her arm around his shoulders. He does not move away. She hugs him.

"It's going to be all right, Hank," she tells him again.

"I'm worried it won't be," he says.

Chapter Eleven

KAZU'S MOTHER, Etsu, a pragmatic woman, accepted Jesus Christ as her Savior and lit incense to the Buddha as well. She wanted nothing left to chance about her final destination. It was Alice who converted Etsu, and Alice who over time talked Etsu out of the Buddhist part of the bargain, convincing the old woman she could not play both sides without offending one of them. Alice had intoned, a bit ominously...*since the Buddha isn't actually around anymore.* Leaving implications for the older woman to wonder about, which she did, and died peacefully with her hands clasped over a Bible and the hospital room smelling of Lysol, not incense.

Kazu was happy his mother's faith made her fearless at death. But he never felt comfortable with religion. He told Alice he believed, because it was what she wanted to hear, but when she searched his eyes, Kazu knew from her eyes that she did not find what she was looking for. It was the eyes, Alice told him, how she will recognize her brothers and sisters on the Day of Judgement, when their graves opened and they stepped forth in perfect, shining bodies while the graves of nonbelievers remained closed. Kazu wondered why she wouldn't recognize her brothers and sisters simply from their graves opening and them stepping forth, while the graves of others did not, and not need to find something in their eyes. But this he decided not to ask.

There were questions he did ask, especially about God's intentions. Why must she, a believer, suffer? Why not the atheists in the world, the liars, the murderers? Why does God not reserve illness and pain for the evildoers in life? Alice closed her eyes and nodded with a gentle smile. She was always pleased to have a ready answer.

"You need faith to understand. Faith is the key that opens the door."

"But why the sickness?"

"It's not sickness. It's a test that makes me stronger."

"But your pain. The medicines don't work anymore."

"Only God can take away pain."

"Sometimes you are in bed for months."

"A gift of solitude that brings me closer to Him."

Kazu wishes he could believe, if only to be closer to Alice. To share the parts of her life that without belief are closed to him. Beliefs he will never know and therefore parts of her he will never understand. He found an unfinished letter Alice had written to someone in her church.

Dear Edna,

My son Hank is a good boy and agreed that what young people do in England is their business, but here, in America, males have short hair, like his father.

My daughter Ruth and I had a talk about duty. I shared with her the story of St. Catherine of Siena as we heard over the radio from our Reverend last weekend. Ruth understands. God is opening her eyes.

I have learned something about physical pain. It is powerful. When it is upon me, I lose myself. In pain it is difficult to be loving and kind. It is difficult to feel the love of my family. Pain pulls me away. I curl into a ball and weep, praying for the pain to end. Instead, it is the love I have that ends. The love for my family ends. It takes all my strength to not cry out. I despair except for the Love of God. Of all, more than even my children, only He remains.

Kazu doesn't understand. Did she stop loving them? Her religion is a mystery. He has seen it in others. In battle, soldiers knelt in the dirt, wringing their hands, grasping onto something not visible to him. But he had his own belief, a pragmatic one. It was this: don't let the other guys down. That was all. What drove him to his feet and forward was terror and anger, not faith. As to the spirit, what happens after death, he did not get a chance to find out. But Alice, Alice is different. He watches as she lies nearly still in the hospital bed, her hands folded on top of each other over her heart. She says she knows. Her chest rises and falls beneath the thin blanket.

Still in his work clothes, Kazu jolts from a kind of sleep. He rubs his eyes and counts the lengthening seconds of her breaths. He leans forward, resting his arms on his knees in the dim light of a small bedside lamp, as he used to do, listening to the advice she liked to give about the children. A nurse brings him the hairbrush he requested and he gently brushes Alice's hair, thinking of how the children will see her when she is dead. What will it be like to put his hand on Alice and find her body has cooled? *A flock of angels in white robes will carry away my soul*, she once said. He had nodded, not saying what he really thought: a flock of angels in white robes is what a child needs to hear, not an adult. People say all kinds of things. When Melon was in the hospital after breaking three ribs in a car wreck and hopped up on pain killers, he mumbled in front of his wife and children, "Brigitte Bardot, Brigitte Bardot, oh how I love thee, Brigitte Bardot." It was hard not to laugh. Especially when Melon said, "Oh how I love thee." He and Melon's family pretended not to hear. But Melon wasn't dying. Does dying, as they say, unroll the past like a newsreel? It didn't for him when he came to for a moment after the mortar hit. All he saw was a circle of dirty faces staring at, he didn't know it then, his spilled guts looping out of his stomach. He watches Alice, wondering if she is seeing her life pass, or dreaming. What does she dream? Her face is calm, only the rise and fall of her slight breath. Her breathing is peaceful, unlike when she is in pain. An image comes to mind of that day in Chicago. She came to buy a fish. The feeling he had when their eyes met. He knew. That's all it was, as ordinary as that. And now here they are. A week ago they celebrated her thirty-fifth birthday. And now the doctor says she will not last the night.

"Hold Mommy's hand."

They descend into the creek. Ruth walks cautiously by Alice's side, her small hand in her mother's. Hank stumbles, but Alice catches him up. At the bottom she lets go of their hands.

"Find a rock like this. Round and flat."

The children search the shore.

"Like this, Mommy?"

"Yes, Hank. Perfect. Hold the rock like this, squat way down..." Alice slings the rock. They watch it skip across the water.

"Try!"

They do, and Alice says, "Perfect, Ruth. Good work, Hank!"

On another day they go to the creek for tadpoles. Alice carries a quart jar. The tide is low and they wade through the shallows. They look in pools and catch the black dots wiggling among the weeds and green moss.

"We'll put them in our pond and they'll become frogs."

"What's over there, Mommy?"

"It's the drain tunnel."

"Can we look?"

They go to the large opening. Daylight penetrates the darkness a few yards inside.

"A monster!" Ruth yells.

Hank screams and the two children run away.

Alice sees they wait for her nearby, holding each other's hands, turned sideways and looking back at her. She stays a moment longer, staring into the dark. A cool wind blows from within.

She is floating.

She always catches more fish than Kazu. It is she who teaches the children how to hold the long poles and where to cast in the surf. Ruth is first to reel one in, and then Hank. They hold them up, side by side.

"Mine's bigger," says Ruth.

"Mine is second biggest," Hank says, and everybody laughs.

"I'll show you kids how to clean fish," Kazu says.

Alice watches him squat with the children where the ocean rushes up the sand. Beyond them waves crash loudly. She gathers pieces of driftwood and makes a small fire. She watches as smoke trails upwards and blows away in the ocean breeze that ruffles her hair.

She sighs from a vague memory of pain. She is not sure from where it comes.

As Ruth and Hank grow, they come to Alice and tell her of their days. She listens and praises and encourages them. When they have troubles, they come to her again, and she soothes them. She volunteers at their schools. At night she reads them bedtime stories of foolish squirrels, grumpy owls, and talking mice.

Hank is a natural at sports. Each season he is among the star players. At every game, Alice cheers him on.

"Go, Hank, go!!!" Leaping to her feet and yelling so loudly the other parents laugh.

At the end of the game, she watches as teammates and coaches pat him on the back.

"Way to go, Hank!"

Ruth is envious. "Why isn't there a league for girls?"

Ruth seeks her advice about boys and Alice tells her everything, even that her first crush was Kazu's brother, Hank, killed in the war.

"Was it strange to marry Dad, Hank's brother?"

"It didn't seem strange."

"Did you marry Dad because he reminded you of Hank?"

"No!" Then, a moment later, Alice says, "Well, I'm not sure."

"Sounds like yes."

"I don't know. No. Wait. I do know. No!" she says. They laugh, and she is glad Ruth's laughter sounds like hers.

In the evenings, after the children go to bed, Alice and Kazu sit on the couch together. She leans against him.

"Both will go to college."

"Yes."

"They must go to college. I'll get a job, too."

"My G.I. Bill will help."

"I wonder about Ruth? She's so smart."

"She's smarter than me. That makes her the smartest," Kazu says.

"Very funny." Alice punches him in the ribs.

She remembers Kazu, always wisecracking.

"And Hank?"

"A doctor."

She nods, her head on Kazu's shoulder.

"A community doctor. Like Kiyonaga."

"I'm sleepy," Alice says.

They go to bed and make love. Sleepy and floating. She remembers how wonderful. The feel of his smooth body against hers. As Kazu sleeps afterwards, Alice lies awake, feeling she has forgotten something important. It bothers her. What is it? She imagines a list of things she is supposed to do tomorrow. Everything is in order. Yet there is something.

Their days pass like this, then years. Ruth attends medical school and meets a Japanese American boy she marries. Hank, to everyone's surprise, becomes a dentist, and marries his assistant, a girl from a family they have known since camp. Alice and Kazu become grandparents. The years pass, their children and grandchildren are well and happy. No tragedies occur.

One day, when Alice is very old, she sits in a lawn chair by the willow tree. It is early summer. The sun is bright and warm, but not too hot. A breeze comes from the ocean carrying the smell of saltwater. Kazu is trimming the iris plants. "Later," Alice thinks, "I will weed the backyard garden."

They are at the end of their lives. She can feel it. Her vision plays tricks. There are shadows and shapes just off to the side, people she has known, now dead. They ignore or don't seem to notice her. They go about their business as if alone. She has lived a long time. The good things of her life are simple things. The tall eucalyptus trees, Kazu kneeling in the flower bed, the dirt road, the pale green of willow leaves swaying in the breeze. Overhead, a whirling cloud of seagulls appear, their white bodies and cries fill the air. "Incoming tide," she thinks. The gulls follow it from the ocean.

She hears a shout from their grandchildren, Keiko and Tadashi, who appear at the top of the creek bank, racing each other to where she sits.

"*Obasan!* We found a cave!"

"You did?"

"Yes, down in the creek."

"It's dark inside, and scary!"

"Be careful," she wants to say, but a breath that is not her own rushes through her like a wind. She is lifted by a dreamy, floating sensation that carries her away. Above the grandchildren still talking and gesturing to her, above herself that she sees is still sitting in the lawn chair listening, above Kazu kneeling in the dirt, above the yard and rooftop and trees, she finds herself in front of the cavernous drain tunnel that empties stormwater into the creek. She looks inside and it is dark, just as they said. A metal gate closes off the opening, but she easily passes through. Still floating, she drifts into the cool shadows. Further on is complete darkness. She goes into it without fear.

She takes a breath and opens her eyes. In the dim light a man is weeping. At first she doesn't know him. Then Alice remembers where she is, who the man is that sits beside her with a bowed head.

She watches him cry and wants to tell him not to, that it is okay. There is no reason to cry. Now she remembers who she is waiting for. She has woken from a dream of another life. How vivid, how wonderful. A dream, a beautiful dream, a temptation. How false it was. But she did not fail. She is grateful for her life, the one she has lived. "Thank you," she whispers. This life. Her illness, the suffering. All of it. "Thank you."

"Yes," she thinks, "I am ready." There is a memory of pain, but that too fades and is gone.

Alice closes her eyes. She sighs a final time.

Kazu, hearing her, looks up.

Chapter Twelve

THE TRUCK won't start. Kazu takes off his jacket and gives it to Ruth to hold, rolls up the sleeves of his white shirt, and opens the hood to fiddle with wires and the carburetor. Waiting in the cab is Ruth wearing a dark gray dress and Hank in a new suit a size too large for him. Kazu gets the engine running and goes back inside to wash his hands. "They can't start without us," he says as they bump down the dirt road. They find the last space in the small church parking lot. When they enter the nave, all faces turn and the room quiets. They walk in silence down the aisle to the front row.

The new pastor hadn't known Alice. He visited with Kazu the night before and took notes about her life. Ruth told Hank the old, white-haired pastor asked questions and drank several glasses of whisky with their father. As the pastor speaks, Hank can only stare at his mother's closed casket, a wreath of flowers on top. The pastor tells the congregation how well he knew Alice, how much Alice loved her husband, Kazu, and their daughter, Ruth. But he fails to mention Hank, who is sitting next to Ruth, and the pastor stares at him from the pulpit in confusion.

A line of cars follow Kazu's truck and the hearse to a cemetery in San Pedro. It is warm and Hank is already uncomfortable. He takes off his jacket and lets it sit crumpled in his lap. Ruth takes his jacket and folds it neatly for him. Lining the cemetery street are shade trees and dwarf palms. Kazu, Ruth, and Hank walk between bronze plaques set into the well-kept grass, Hank glancing down at names on the rows of headstones. It makes him think of the Hollywood Walk of Fame. Chairs are set around the gravesite. There is a mound of earth and a tarp covering a hole in the ground.

The pastor lifts his chin and talks in a strained voice, the skin of his neck withered and loose. Like a turkey, Hank thinks. The sun beats down and in his new jacket Hank begins to sweat. When the pastor is finished speaking the family is summoned to place a rose on the casket. When it is his turn, Hank is aware of everyone watching. Judging him, he knows. He remembers once hearing a lady say, "I don't know how Alice can rest with her son so noisy and loud."

Returning to the truck, someone calls his name. Three boys dressed neatly in black suits run up. It is the Three Kings. They come to a stop in front of him with solemn faces.

"We're sorry about your mom."

They each shake his hand.

They wait a moment, then one says, "We haven't seen you at practice."

"I'm not in the league this year."

"It's fun. You should give it another try!"

Hank looks at their faces. He sees kindness and goodwill.

"I'm not good at sports."

"We'll help you."

All three nod as if they have discussed it already.

"It's just practice. If you practice, you get good."

"My dad practices with me. Otherwise, I wouldn't be any good, either."

"We could practice with you."

"I don't know. Maybe next year."

"Okay, next year. Be ready!"

"Are you guys coming to the house?"

"Aw, no, we have a game."

They shake hands again and run back the way they came.

He sees Ruth talking to a Caucasian boy with dark hair. A short distance away is Shirley Carson, standing with her hands folded in front of herself as if waiting in line. Hank sits in the cab of the truck, leaving the door open. He watches Kazu shake hands with the pastor and hand him an envelope. A figure trots over. It is Tak.

"Hey, Hank. So sorry about your mom."

"It's okay."

Tak is wearing his black leather jacket with a white shirt and tie.

"You coming to the house?"

"Yeah. My mom's gonna drop me off. See you there."

"Okay. See you."

Kazu doesn't speak on the way home. He knows Ruth and Hank are waiting for him to say something. He runs a phrase or two through his mind, trying to find words to bring them comfort.

"Let's roll down the windows," is all he can manage. They listen to the freeway noise.

He drives the truck around into the backyard. As they enter the house there are a group of women already inside. They have volunteered to take everything out of his hands, to prepare food, organize chairs and tables on the patio, and give smaller tasks to Ruth and Hank to keep them busy. Kazu thanks them and leaves them to their work. He goes to Alice's room and opens the door. He leans against the doorframe, staring at the empty bed.

How many funerals has he attended and afterwards went to the house of the bereaved to eat? He knew this day would come but he never tried to imagine it. He takes a deep breath and puts on a face to make his guests comfortable.

In the living room he shakes hands and accepts condolences, then guides his guests into the kitchen, where women take the food and flowers and usher the guests outside to the small patio to eat and drink and visit with people they haven't seen since the last funeral.

When the time seems right, Kazu goes around to make sure everybody has what they want. That task finished, he joins his Friday night poker gang and the doctor, Mitz Kiyonaga, at a table. Kazu sees they are sitting in the same arrangement they do on game night. For some reason it annoys him.

Dr. Kiyonaga pours a little whiskey into a glass and gives it to Kazu. He stands and begins to say something, but Melon loudly announces, "Hey Kaz, bonita are running."

"That's good," Kazu says.

"I want to try my Daiwa reel."

Dr. Kiyonaga sits down without finishing what he was saying.

"Kaz, let's go fishing!"

"Pack a lunch, some beer!" Hash says.

"Shall we?" Melon says. Everyone at the table murmurs in agreement.

"The creek's not bad off the north jetty."

They look at Kazu expectantly.

"Sure," he says.

"Okay then!" Eto pours drinks around from the bottle.

They sip their whiskey, hold their glasses up to look inside and swirl the ice cubes.

"Good stuff," Joe Yamada says.

"Hmm," says Melon.

"Did I see a box of tacos?" Hash wonders, twisting around to look at the table where the food is.

"From Tito's."

"And a box from Johnny's. Pastrami sandwiches. Can't beat Johnny's."

The men drink, stretch, and yawn. Eto lights a cigar.

"Joe, tell Kaz about the Golden Duck," says Hash.

"I went last night. Had scallops with Chinese vegetables. Stayed up half the night in the benjo."

"I heard their head cook stabbed a customer in the face with a serving fork."

"Is that so?"

"It's what I heard."

"From who?"

"Chinese guy I know, works at Hughes."

"The almond chicken has a special—"

"I want to say something," Dr. Kiyonaga interrupts, pushing himself to his feet. Everyone at the table falls silent. He stares at them. "Alice was a good, kind woman. A brave woman. She did her best to raise a family. I don't know of many people who could have suffered with the grace that she did. She never whined to me about her illness. Kazu says the same. She never complained." He picks up the bottle and pours a little splash of whiskey, carefully, like medicine, into everyone's glass. "She was sick a long time. In terrible pain. Only Kaz knows how bad it was. She's at peace now. Let's drink to her." Kazu bows his head. Dr. Kiyonaga pats Kazu on the shoulder.

The men are silent, sipping their whiskey, not looking at each other. They glance at Kazu, who is wiping his eyes.

Dr. Kiyonaga excuses himself.

After a few moments, Hash says, "So, fishing?"

Melon pushes back his chair. "I'm going to get some more teri chicken wings. Anybody?"

"Bring me some, and a taco," Eto says. "Kaz?" He lifts the bottle.

"No. I want to check on Ruth." Kazu blows his nose into a handkerchief, leaves his whiskey on the table and makes his way over to where Ruth is sitting with the Carson girl.

"Hi. Shirley, right?"

She stands up and shakes his hand. "I'm so sorry about your wife."

"Thank you."

"My parents send their well wishes. They're sorry they couldn't be here."

"Please thank them for me. Ruth, make a plate for Shirley to take home."

"I will."

"You don't have to!"

"It's for your parents, not you," Ruth says.

Someone calls Kazu's name. It's the owner of the plant nursery and his wife. As he joins them he sees Hank and Tak going in the direction of the backyard. When he can get away he follows, wondering what they are up to. But now the boys are on the road along the creek, walking together in their dark suits. They must have gone from the backyard across the fields. "Going to smoke cigarettes," he thinks, wanting one himself.

That night is Kazu's enema night. He absentmindedly examines the thick scars from war wounds on his body, tracing them with his finger and pressing around the colostomy that never fails to remind him of old, raw meat. He puts on a bathrobe and goes into the kitchen. Through the window he looks across the patio and sees a line of light under Hank's door. He opens the refrigerator where plates of food are covered by tin foil and wax paper. He reads the little notes taped on by the women to identify what's under the wrappings. He's not hungry, though. He doesn't know what he wants.

When loved ones die they leave a lot of work for the living. Files to be searched through, papers to complete. Insurance forms, death certificates, funeral home business, cemetery arrangements, bills to pay, thank you notes to write, a koden list to update. There is a beneficial side, though. All the work keeps his mind off Alice. It seems unfair he can't be left alone to grieve, but these mundane tasks must be accomplished and they draw him back into the world.

He can sleep where she slept.

In the semidarkness he crawls into her bed and rests his head on her pillow. Thin curtains shift in the breeze by the open window. Moonlight seeps into the room. He thinks about her days, drifting in and out of wakefulness and sleep. Here. Her head lay here. He clutches the pillow.

He remembers the evenings, sitting on her bed with her and talking. Alice's questions about Ruth and Hank, if they were happy, what difficulties they faced at school, their interests, what kind of friendships they had. She wanted to know everything.

What could he say? Ruth follows the rules and does well in school, but her face is pinched and worried-looking and she's afraid to leave the house. And Hank. He kicked and broke the closet door in his room for no reason! He punched a hole in the wall and acted like it was nothing. He was supposed to fix it but the hole is still there. Eto saw him smoking cigarettes. He is failing most of his classes. The teachers send notes, he doesn't do his homework. When Kazu scolds him he nods but doesn't listen.

There wasn't any point in telling her that.

In the morning Kazu sits at the kitchen table writing thank you notes. Ruth comes from her room. "Hi, Dad," she says. Kazu grunts softly. The water is still hot on the stove and Ruth makes tea, looking over her shoulder at what Kazu is doing. He does not ask for help, but she finds a pen and sits across from him. There is a large stack of notes, stamps and envelopes, and an open ledger they push back and forth. He looks at her a couple of times and smiles.

A while later Hank appears in the kitchen and opens the refrigerator. He finds musubi on a paper plate covered with foil.

He takes a bite from one.

"Why don't they make musubi that's good the next day?"

"The rice dries out in the fridge," Ruth says.

"So? Why don't they fix it? And where's the ume?"

"It's always in the last part you eat."

"Why is that?"

He takes another rice ball and stuffs it in his mouth. He shoves the paper plate back into the fridge.

"I'm going," he mumbles. "Bye."

The front door slams behind him.

Ruth looks at Kazu who is bent over, concentrating on writing an address. His face has a stiff, blank expression that Ruth knows. He could have asked Hank to help with the notes, but their father does not ask for help. If he has to ask for help he'd rather not have it. If people pay attention, and if they care, asking for help is not needed. That's what he thinks. If not, if they don't care and don't help, he becomes angry and pretends he is not.

In the days since Alice died the three of them pass each other as though half asleep. Not even a glance to acknowledge that she is dead. There is no family gathering, no words from Kazu. Is this normal? Ruth wonders. When the funeral is over do other families go on as usual? Do normal families comfort each other? Their father has no comforting words, only gaman. Unspoken, but it's there in his eyes, as if his own perseverance can be forced upon them. Kazu once complained that Hank hasn't learned anything from him. But Ruth can see what Hank is learning. It seems wrong to her, but not having children, who is she to know better?

When the notes are written, the envelopes addressed and stamped, Kazu collects them in neat stacks and wraps them with rubber bands. He sighs.

"Thank you, Ruth," he says.

"You're welcome, Dad."

Chapter Thirteen

Ruth sits on the bench near Miss Parker's room, waiting for Shirley to join her. The thought crosses her mind that she will end up eating lunch alone like a fool. But here is Shirley, walking up the path. They sit together, quietly glancing at each other. Ruth takes two green apples from her bag. Shirley smiles. A couple of boys walk by and wave.

Shirley sighs. "I've been helping Mom pack Dad's stuff."

"He's really leaving?"

"Yes."

Ruth pictures Mr. Carson. Tall and thin, his grey observant eyes, his secret life exposed.

"It's a bummer. But not as bad as about your mom."

They are quiet and seem at a loss. Before, they always had plenty to talk about.

Miss Parker walks by, fixing her hair, and smiles at Ruth. They watch her go in the direction of the parking lot.

"So tell me," Ruth says. "What happened with Molly?"

"Oh, it's so stupid."

"Tell me."

Shirley looks Ruth in the eyes.

"Connor and Molly took me to a party, and one of their friends started telling jokes. That's all."

"What kind of jokes?"

"About Japanese people."

"Oh."

"I tried to be a good sport. I laughed."

"Did Connor and Molly laugh?"

"Connor looked at me and made a face, but he kept laughing. Molly was practically shrieking."

Ruth nods.

"Connor told his friend that the jokes weren't very nice, but Molly said, 'No, no! Don't feel bad!' That's what she said! Then Connor said, 'Don't worry, he tells worse jokes at school.'"

"He said don't worry?"

"Yeah. What's that supposed to mean?"

"Why didn't he tell his friend to shut up?"

"It would ruin the party."

A group of students run by chasing a dog.

"I wondered if those things happened to you," Ruth says.

"You did?" Shirley studies Ruth's face.

They stare at each other.

"Yes."

"Hmm. Now you know." Shirley rolls the apple back and forth between her hands. "Later I thought it was my fault. But it's not. I don't like them anymore."

The bell rings and students walk noisily to class.

"We friends again?" Shirley says.

Ruth smiles. "Yes."

"Meet here tomorrow?"

"I can't. I see someone during lunch."

"You do? A boy?"

"Yes."

"Who?"

"I'll call you tonight."

"Yes! Call me!"

"I will," Ruth says.

Ruth decided to lie to Shirley about what she does at lunchtime. Her special place, her refuge, she will not give it up, not even for Shirley. "Is something wrong with me?" she wonders. To prefer being alone with her sketch pad, attempting to draw images of her hands over and over. It is odd.

"I'm odd," she thinks.

That night over the telephone, Ruth tells Shirley, as matter-of-factly as she can, what she lets John do during science class.

"Oh my god, really? In class?"

Ruth is pleased by the shocked tone in Shirley's voice.

"Yes. We sit in the back and no one can see us."

"How far do you let him go?"

"Shirley!"

"Come on! How far?"

"He stays at my knee."

"Just the knee?"

"Yes."

"Does he try to go further?"

"Every day."

"He does? What do you do?"

"I put my hand on his. And he stops."

"He does?"

"He knows if he misbehaves, no more knee."

"Oh, my god," Shirley says.

When she gets off the phone with Shirley, Ruth smiles.

For weeks after Alice dies, Hank continues to come home directly from school. There is no one here, the house is his, but he feels more a prisoner than ever. When Alice was alive everything had to be done quietly. Eating, reading comic books, sneaking into Ruth's room to snoop through her things. Now that Alice is gone he doesn't have to be quiet. He turns up the volume on the TV, he yells to hear his voice. He listens to a music radio station while he makes food in the kitchen. Yet he still winces when he accidentally bangs pans together. The house is empty, his noise bothers no one, but he is self-conscious of everything he does, as if the presence of his mother is more powerful than ever and gives orders from behind the closed door of her room into every corner of the house.

He begins staying after school as he has always wanted, to run free with other students past classrooms where teachers are bent over their desks, grading papers. Sometimes they stop to visit with teachers they like.

Mr. Canetti, the leader of the Garden Club, is a favorite. If his door is open it means he is inside. If closed, he is at the garden.

As Mr. Canetti promised, the Garden Club raised money to build a greenhouse and barbecue area. Almost daily in class he talks about what a success the garden is for students. Hank goes after school one day to take a look. The greenhouse is small, about the size of his bedroom, with whitewashed glass. He asks Mr. Canetti if the whitewash interferes with sunlight.

"It's not sunlight. We have plenty of sunlight." Mr. Canetti lifts his arms to the sky. "We have so much light it will burn the plants. It's for consistency of temperature. The whitewash makes it heat better, and uniformly."

The barbecue pit is made of red brick and looks like a fireplace.

"These are special bricks," Mr. Canetti says, patting them. "Ordinary bricks will crack from the heat. These will not. See what a nice job the masons did?"

Part of the money Mr. Canetti raised went to pay for professional bricklayers.

"And over here. Look at all the work we have done."

He shows Hank the growing area. "See how we built mounds instead of rows? It's called 'raised beds' and it's more efficient." Oblong mounds of dirt lie in rows waiting for shoots to be transplanted from the greenhouse. Some are planted already with radishes.

"They look like graves," Hank says.

"In a few weeks we will have our party."

"Oh boy!"

Mr. Canetti looks at Hank sadly. "Hank, you had the chance to join, but for whatever reason, you did not. Sorry, but the party is for Garden Club members only."

"Oh."

"You understand, it is only fair. It wouldn't be right for non-members to come to the party when the members have done all the work. Do you remember the hen that baked the bread and none of the other animals helped?"

"No. I don't know what you're talking about."

"The hen said she would bake bread, but none of the animals cared to help her, so she did it all herself. When it was done, it smelled delicious and all the animals wanted a taste. But the hen told them, 'No one else would help me, so I did it all by myself. Now I will eat it all by myself.' And the hen did. Do you see the lesson of the story?"

"Yeah. Don't trust a fucking hen."

"What did you say?"

"Nothing."

"I think you better leave now, Hank."

On Saturday, Hank wakes up late. He gets out of bed and stands in the doorway in his underwear, looking outside. It is already too hot, and he feels lazy. Tak is with his dad for the weekend and Hank does not feel like wandering around by himself. He thinks for a moment about the girl at the mirror store and if he should walk by to see if she is there. He's not sure if the boy who punched him really is her brother or if he was only pretending to be. He decides it is better not to take a chance.

He dresses and goes into the kitchen where he sees Ruth and ignores her. She gave him a hug that night when Alice went to the hospital, and he felt close to her again. But afterwards she seemed to expect he would bare his life to her or something dumb like that. She looks at him the way Dr. Kiyonaga does when he asks if something hurts. It is fine for a doctor, but from Ruth it is annoying. Their father is working, as he does every Saturday, which is good. It means Hank can relax and not have to pretend he is doing something constructive.

He reads comic books. Later, he walks in the back yard not knowing what he wants, and in a vague disinterested way lingers by the wood pile and thinks about catching a lizard. There are a couple of blue bellies sunning themselves. He looks carefully at their tails, but that was a long time ago. The lizards he and Ruth experimented on are surely dead. The lizards make him remember those days, how he and Ruth used to play together. He remembers the cat with her kittens and the two boys. How tough Ruth was, killing a mud hen to feed the cat, then kicking and punching the older boys when they threatened the kittens. It's hard to believe she was ever like that. What happened to her? She always led the way. Her ideas were the most fun and he never minded following her. In fact, he liked it! Now she is docile and boring. He walks to the field and searches the ground where he thinks the kittens were, as if after all these years he might find something. Kicking at the crumbly, dry dirt of the field, he looks over to the school. He might as well walk around it. There isn't anything better to do.

In the parking lot he sees the hole in the wall. "One more time," he thinks to himself. He remembers what Mr. Nice said about the weekend janitor, so he will be careful. It's better he's here alone and not with Tak, who always makes too much noise. He gets on his belly and crawls through.

Now he is on school grounds. It is empty, eerily quiet.

It is only a few weeks until summer vacation. He thinks about the past school year, walking the halls with throngs of other students, stopping at his locker, going to classes. Here's the small courtyard where he saw the girl. He remembers how sunlight shone on her hair and how her beauty hypnotized him. Now he goes to where she stood, as if something, a scent, an essence of her, might linger. From there he wanders into the lunch area. He walks by the student store where the pretty girl sold him a jockstrap on the second day of the new school year. He can still picture her. He wonders if she remembers or ever thinks about him.

Not intending to, he finds himself by the Garden Club. There is a chain-link fence and gate. A padlock hangs on the gate but is not secured, as if someone went away but expected to be right back. He opens the gate and steps inside. Mr. Canetti calls it "The Secret Garden." Hank thinks he calls it that because hedges conceal it from the rest of the school.

He walks around the Garden Club area, feeling like an outsider. He goes to the planting area and squats down to poke his finger at a plant in the mound. He pulls it up. It is a radish. He remembers growing these in elementary school. He rubs the dirt off the small red bulb and bites into it. It is crisp and peppery.

Someone left a hoe lying on the ground. He swings it around his head a few times, pretending it is a samurai sword. There is the tool shed. "I'll put it away for them," he thinks.

He opens the door to the small shed and leans the hoe against the wall. There are a lot of tools: shovels, rakes, an axe, a sledgehammer, coiled watering hoses, and various clippers, all neatly arranged. He recognizes them, the same tools his father uses. He shuts the door.

He wanders over to the brick barbecue. "Fire bricks," he says aloud. Then opens the door to the small greenhouse and goes inside.

There are narrow wooden tables against the glass walls. On the tables are trays, and in the trays are small, separate containers with a single plant in each. Little, weak-looking plants.

It is warm. Very warm. Hank looks at the whitewashed glass.

He goes back to the tool shed and returns, unhurriedly, with the sledgehammer. "It's heavy," he thinks. He likes the long wooden handle.

Gripping the handle with both hands he swings it at the wooden tables. They break easily. The weight of the hammer is enough to wreck the tables, destroy the trays, crush the plants. He smashes everything. It is easy. He examines the twisted, broken angles of the wooden starter frames, and the clumps of black soil and pale green plants with white roots that are scattered randomly across the cement floor as if a small tornado had landed. "Looks better now," Hank says aloud. Then he uses the hammer to break the glass panes of the walls. It is fun holding the handle and ramming the head through the panes. He shatters everything, enjoying the crinkly explosions of breaking glass. He looks at the roof. He imagines shoving the hammer upwards, over his head, but that seems dangerous. He goes outside to the barbecue and swings the hammer until the red brick barbecue is broken into rubble. It takes a while and he rests several times. It is hard work! Now he has something to throw. From outside he tosses bricks onto the glass roof of the greenhouse, watching the sharp glass rain inside. Were he in there he'd be sliced to pieces. Good thing he was smart enough not to be.

Hank surveys what he has accomplished and finds it is good.

He drags the hammer to the growing area. All he need do is lift the heavy sledgehammer by the end of the handle and drop it on the plants, over and over, and he can smash them all. He looks at the grave-like mounds in rows next to each other, imagining them flattened and destroyed. "I will let the radishes grow," he decides.

He returns the sledgehammer to its place in the tool shed, closes the doors, and takes a final look at what he has done. A single brick stands upright on the broken wall of the barbecue. It offends him, that brick. He walks over and kicks it off. Satisfied, he leaves the Garden Club area, securing the padlock on the gate as it should have been done before. "People should be more careful," he thinks. For the first time in years he feels light, happy.

That evening he sits on the bed in his room, considering whether to go into the back yard and smoke a cigarette Tak gave him. He doesn't like smoking, it still makes him dizzy and nauseous if he smokes more than one in a row. But Tak told him to keep trying and after a while it will get better.

Someone knocks on the door. At first he is frightened, wondering if it is the police. Then he knows from the light tapping it is Ruth. She taps on doors with the same shy, *Forgive me for bothering you* way she does everything in life.

"Can I come in?"

"What do you want?"

"Hank, can we talk?"

Hank steps back. He pulls the wobbly chair from the desk and sits. He points to the bed.

"What?" he says.

Ruth puts her hands together in her lap and stares at him.

Hank sighs and looks away. He wonders if their father is home. If not, he wants to go in the kitchen and make something to eat.

"Dad home?"

"Yes, he just got home."

"I need food."

"Can we talk about Mom?"

Hank shrugs.

"Other families would talk."

"I'm hungry."

"Hank, come sit with me?"

Maybe if he does she will make him a sandwich.

She pats the bed at her side for him to sit. She puts her arm around his shoulders. When he doesn't pull away she puts her other arm around Hank and hugs him, resting her head on the top of his.

He lets her. He's always liked how she smells. He remembers liking to be close to her when they were little.

Words come out his mouth before he knows what he is saying. He doesn't know why he says what he does, because he's not thinking of anything. He says, "I made Mom sick."

"What do you mean?"

"I dunno. Dad told me. He said me being born made Mom sick."

Ruth shakes her head. "That's not true, Hank."

"That's what Dad said."

"No. Dr. Kiyonaga told Dad if Mom got pregnant again, she might not recover."

"Yeah. That was me."

"Hank. It was Dad."

"How was it Dad?"

"Because Dr. Kiyonaga warned him. But Mom got pregnant anyway. That was Dad. It was his fault. Not yours."

"What are you talking about? You can't say that about Dad."

"Hank, it wasn't your fault."

"It's me who was born. You can't say that about Dad!"

Hank jerks to his feet, hands searching for something to grab. He yanks at the desk and the drawer falls out and everything spills to the floor. He kicks through the pile looking for something, a knife, a screwdriver, a stabbing tool. Not to hurt Ruth, but himself. Hurting himself to make her sorry for what she said. Stab himself in the leg, that's a good place to start. Here's a pencil. It makes him think of Tak's eye. That must have hurt. Tak never said it did, but it must have hurt. Hank grips the yellow wooden pencil in his fist, staring at the black tip, trying to imagine it, but he can't. He loses the desire to stab himself. He sees Ruth watching him silently from the bed. He kicks the chair. It flies against the wall with a bang. Ruth jumps up and leaves the room, looking over her shoulder at him with wide, frightened eyes. "That's better," he thinks. "Now she gets the message."

Not knowing what else to do, he grabs the chair off the floor and shakes it violently.

Later he goes to the back yard and smokes a cigarette. He stares across the fields, barely visible in the evening shadows. Remembering, he puts his hand in his pocket. It's the same pants he's been wearing all week and there it is, the slip of torn paper Tak wrote the message in a bottle on. He unfolds it and looks. He can't read in the dark, but he remembers the words. He rubs the paper between his fingers. When Tak wrote it, Hank thought it was funny. But not anymore. He crumples it up and lights it on fire.

On Monday, in Social Studies, Mr. Canetti's eyes behind his glasses glisten with tears as he talks about the Garden Club. He describes how vandals destroyed what had taken the Garden Club an entire year to build. He says he cannot understand this evilness, cannot understand the malicious disregard for the happiness of others.

"It meant so much to me and to students."

A girl in the class starts to cry.

"What kind of parents does this person have?" Mr. Canetti asks. "If anybody knows or hears anything, please tell me in private. I will not reveal your name." He sweeps his eyes across the class as though seeking the vandal among them.

Students turn their heads from side to side, looking at each other with suspicion. Hank, sitting in the middle row, does the same.

During lunch Hank sees students walking in the direction of the Garden Club. He follows them. The gate is padlocked, so they lean against the fence and peer through the hedges. Hank does, too.

"Who would do that?" he hears a student say.

"I hear it was someone from the housing projects," another student says.

Hank walks back to the lunch area and sits on a bench against the wall. The tables and benches are jammed with students chattering and screaming. Mr. Nice and other teachers who usually walk around on lunch patrol instead gather in a small group. They talk and glance over to the Garden Club area. Hank goes to the student store to see if the same girl is there from the beginning of the year. She is not, but he buys a Payday anyway and sits on the bench where he was before and eats the candy bar for lunch.

The bell rings. He remains where he is and watches as other students rush to their classes. Mr. Nice and the teachers walk past. They ignore him.

"They don't know," he thinks.

After school he waits outside the front entrance to see if the mirror store girl will be there. Cars pull to the curb with parents staring from behind the steering wheels. Their old, anxious faces all look the same. Groups of students surge forward, laughing and talking loudly. He doesn't see her. Disappointed, he waits longer. Surely she will appear. Then he sighs. "What's the point?" He wanders back through the entrance gates. He passes near the main office. Without stopping or giving it a thought he turns inside and goes down the hallway where the waxed floor reflects the glaring fluorescent lights. He doesn't ask himself what he's doing. The lady at the counter calls loudly, "Young man, can I help you?" He walks past without answering and opens the door into a small office.

Mr. Nice is sitting at his desk, writing in a notebook. He looks up.

"Tanazaki. What can I do for you?"

Hank stands in front of the desk.

"It was me."

"What was you?"

"The Garden Club."

Mr. Nice puts his pen down.

"You?"

"Yes."

"Who else?"

"No one."

"Just you?"

"Yes."

Mr. Nice stares at him.

"Well, Mr. Tanazaki," Mr. Nice says, leaning back in his chair. "You don't say."

Chapter Fourteen

TAK LOOKS at him in disgust.

"Whatcha do that for?"

"I don't know."

"Oh man, *baka*, you're so stupid. What they going to do?"

"I don't know."

"I can't believe you're so stupid."

"I didn't plan to break anything. It just happened."

"Not that! That sounds fun. I mean telling on yourself."

"I dunno. I felt bad for Mr. Canetti."

"Who's that?"

"The teacher of the Garden Club."

"You felt bad for him?"

"Nah. I guess not. I dunno." Hank puts his hands in his pockets. He looks at Tak and shrugs. They are at the TG&Y. An old woman with a floral scarf tied around her face is coming their way, a wooden cane hanging from the shopping cart she leans on. She pauses and they step aside for her.

That night there is a tapping at his door. Ruth has a plate with a baloney sandwich on it. He stares at the sandwich sullenly, as though it too might be angry with him, and takes the plate from her hands but does not invite her inside. "Thank you," he mumbles. The first words he has spoken to her in a couple of days. He backs into his room and closes the door.

The next afternoon he walks into her room without knocking. He doesn't knock because once it was his room as well.

"What you doing?"

"Just got off the phone with Shirley."

"How's she?"

"Her dad left."

"Yeah."

They both stand, Hank looking at the floor.

"You look like the weight of the world is on your shoulders."

"They're going to send me to juvie."

"You don't know that. Dad says Mr. Nice is thinking about what to do."

"Mr. Nice. He'll send me to juvie for sure."

"Wait and see. Dad says Mr. Nice will let him know this week."

"I can't stand waiting. I know they'll send me to juvie."

"Wait and see, Hank."

The school expels Hank, but with only a few weeks left it doesn't matter. He was failing his classes anyway. Mr. Nice advises that criminal charges not be brought against Hank if he helps repair the damage he has done, as well as attend summer school and make up credit.

When summer school ends at noon Hank goes to the garden club for his first task, to recondition fire bricks, chipping away broken mortar with a mason's hammer so they can be reused. As for the greenhouse, the structural frame is mostly intact. Hank sweeps up the broken glass and salvages as much building material as he can, pulling nails from lumber and carefully removing debris from the frames. If new material is required, Kazu will have to pay for it.

Mr. Nice makes a further deal with Hank.

"Pass both classes and I'll rebuild the barbecue and greenhouse. You'll help me, of course. That way, your father won't have to pay to hire somebody."

"You know how to do that?"

"In addition to chasing knuckleheads like you, I can do useful things."

One day, Tak shows up as Hank and Mr. Nice are working. Hank introduces them.

"So, it's Tak and Tanazaki. Tak, you live around here?"

"Staying with my father for a few weeks."

"Staying with your father, huh? Well, grab some bricks and start cleaning. Here, take my chisel."

"Thanks!"

Mr. Nice watches him for a few minutes.

"Tak, use the other end."

"Oh. Hey! Works better!"

Mr. Nice sighs and shakes his head.

The summer passes. The fire bricks are stacked neatly, cleaned and ready for use. Mr. Nice sweeps the concrete foundation, saying, "It's nice and level. Makes it easier for us. Thanks for not destroying it, Tanazaki."

He shows them how to string line for the bricks. The boys watch. Tak says, "I know a faster way."

"Oh, do you?"

"Put the bricks next to each other. Use the bricks to line up the other bricks. You don't need a string."

"Is that right?"

"Do it like building blocks. I had a set of building blocks and—"

"I see you have a brilliant mind, Tak. One that knows a better way of doing things than people who have done it for years."

Tak grins at Hank and gives him the thumbs up.

"Tell you what. I'll do my old, slow way with the string. And you boys line your bricks up your way. Do it over there. Just to see."

Tak and Hank grab bricks and place them together as fast as they can, checking the corners of each to make sure it lines up with the one before it. Mr. Nice lays his out along the string line, checking the line to the brick. The boys finish quickly.

"Ha! We beat you!" says Tak.

"Yes, you have!" Mr. Nice exclaims.

Tak and Hank strut around their brick wall and then over to where Mr. Nice is still kneeling in the dirt. With his overalls instead of a suit, and old work boots instead of shiny black loafers, Mr. Nice looks like a different person. Not scary, but softer and more friendly. He has dust in his hair. Now he pushes himself up and goes to examine what the boys have done. Tak and Hank look at each other and smirk.

"Yes, you boys are amazing. Already experts at something you've never done before. Oh, wait a minute. Your bricks don't line up. Come over here and see what I mean."

Their bricks are not in a straight line. The wall they built curves to the right and leans over to the side. Mr. Nice uses a mason's level to show them how off-kilter it is.

"Now look at mine." Mr. Nice walks them back to his wall and applies the level. It is perfectly straight in every direction. "There's no mortar, but the wall can already support weight." He moves the top of the brick row from side to side and it sways but remains upright. He barely nudges their wall with his finger and it tips over.

"The string is a reference point. If you go brick by brick, as you two did, the reference point changes with each brick. Just a little, just a sixteenth of an inch, but after a while it grows, and then you have a miserable-looking wall. Like your wall. The string is a constant, always the same reference point to measure from."

"Why do you have to put the string away from the brick?"

"Otherwise bricks touch the string and push it out, change it a little bit, and change the reference point. You boys need to remember this: get a good reference point, prove it's a good one through experience, and stick with it. Going brick by brick building a wall is the same as just going moment to moment building a life. And where do you end up? Somewhere far from where you intended to be. Right, Tanazaki? Find a good reference point. Are you hearing me? I'm not just talking about bricks."

"Okay," Tak says.

"Okay," says Hank, but he isn't sure what Mr. Nice means.

They take the bricks down and return them to the stack. Mr. Nice pounds in stakes for string lines.

"Now we're going to mix the mortar. Get the wheelbarrow from the tool shed. Tanazaki knows where the tool shed is, same place as the sledgehammer. You know very well, don't you, Tanazaki?"

"I know where everything is!"

They rush over and Tak returns with the wheelbarrow, pushing it so fast he hits a bump and it falls over, jamming the end of the handle into his groin.

"Fuck!" he cries. Then looks at Mr. Nice. "Sorry."

"Tak, are you always running a race?"

"What do you mean?"

"Slow down. You'll live longer. Now bring it over here."

Mr. Nice lifts a sack of mortar into the wheelbarrow, splits it open with the point of a shovel and yanks out the paper sack leaving the mortar behind.

"Hank, bring that hose. Turn the water on, just a little bit. No, more than that. Okay, that's about right. Now come here."

The two boys gather around.

"The important thing about mixing mortar is it takes less water than you think. If you add too much water you can always add more mortar, but learn to get it right the first time. What if you overdo the water but don't have extra mortar? You see what I mean?"

"Uh huh."

"Yes, sir."

"Okay. Watch how I do it. Then you try."

It takes several more days, but the barbecue is rebuilt. The three of them stand back and admire it.

"I think we did a better job than those masons," Mr. Nice says.

"Let's cook hot dogs!"

"Tak, I think you've eaten enough hot dogs in your life," Mr. Nice says, laughing.

Tak is quiet.

"Get the greenhouse done and we'll make hot dogs. On me," Mr. Nice says.

Tak smiles.

On the day they finish the greenhouse, Mr. Nice shows up with charcoal, hot dogs, buns, mustard, ketchup, and relish. He also has soda pop on ice and potato chips.

"You boys did a nice job. A pleasure working with you," Mr. Nice tells them.

"We should have invited Mr. Canetti to see what we did."

"Tanazaki, I think you better avoid Mr. Canetti as much as possible. I've arranged for you to have Mrs. Clark for Social Studies next year."

"I was thinking of joining the Garden Club."

Mr. Nice stares at Hank. "Man, you are something else. I caution you against it. Don't even ask. All right. Let's start the charcoal. Tak, get the bag and lighter fluid. Now, you don't want to use too much fluid because it leaves a taste."

After summer school ends and Hank has passed his classes, he and Tak meet to celebrate. They catch a bus to the beach and walk north along the shore to Pacific Ocean Park pier. They go under the pier and climb on the walkways between pilings to smoke a joint and watch the surfers. A dim, greenish light comes from the ocean as it swirls against the barnacled pilings in surges of white foam. The air is cool and thick, smelling of seawater and creosote. The waves crash loudly.

"They call this The Cove, the best surf spot," Tak says.
"I know."
"Look at that dude. He's ripping."
"It's that Chinese guy."
"Asian people, man, the best surfers."
"I thought Hawaiians were."
"They're Asian!"
"Hawaiians are Asian?"
"Yeah! Have you ever seen one? They look kind of Asian."
"I thought Hawaiians were Polynesian, Indonesian, or something."
"That's part of Asia."
"I guess."
"Whaddaya think of this weed?"
Tak puts a roach clip on and they pass it back and forth.
"Look at that dude. He rips, too," says Hank.
"That's Limey. His friends made fun of him all the time for being red-haired and freckled and scrawny. So he lifted weights and took karate. And one day he went nuts and beat the shit outta his old friends and got new ones."
"He beat them up?"
"They deserved it."
"How do you know these guys? You live in Long Beach."
"I hear shit. I heard something else, too. I heard my mom talking on the phone. She wants me to live with relatives in Japan. It's fucked."
"No way."
"She doesn't have money, my dad doesn't have money. Our relatives have a lot of money. I don't wanna go. I hate it there. My relatives are cool, but kids make fun of me cuz I can't speak good."
"That's a bummer, dude."
"Yeah."
Tak takes a pack of cigarettes from his pocket and shakes a couple out. They smoke and watch surfers ride the waves.

"What did Mr. Nice mean about having a string line?" Hank says.
"I dunno. He said 'reference.' What does that mean?"
"I dunno," says Hank.

Chapter Fifteen

SHIRLEY SMILES, polishing the apple from Ruth on her skirt. Her hair is different, she wears it like Ruth does, long and straight, falling past her shoulders, and bangs. They are sitting on their bench having lunch.

"We're going to Hawaii. Mom says I can bring one friend." She looks at Ruth expectantly, her eyebrows raised.

"Gee, I don't know."

"Mom has family there. We won't be tourists. And the boys! So many beautiful boys."

Ruth thinks about John.

"We'll pay for the ticket. Dad has to give us money. Come on. You're going!"

Ruth had been looking forward to the summer when she could spend time with John. But last weekend she saw him at the TG&Y with a girl she recognized from school. They were holding hands, looking through a large window into the store. Ruth was sure John noticed her in the window's reflection but pretended not to. In science class the next day, when John walked into the room he seemed momentarily confused. Ruth sat at another desk, not theirs. John went to their old desk and quietly slipped into his seat as though nothing was different. Ruth exchanged a look with Mrs. Jackson, who stared back, then nodded and began a lesson. Ruth ignored John, who kept his eyes lowered and picked at his fingernails.

"He found someone to give him more than a knee," she told Shirley.

"Good riddance to bad rubbish."

Kazu thought Hawaii was a good idea. "Those buddhaheads are okay. During the war we met at Camp Shelby for training. They didn't like us at first."

"Why?"

Kazu shrugs. "We were different. They thought we acted *high maka maka*. Like big shots. They didn't know about the camps, it didn't happen to them, and we were still in shock, mad at everything. But when they learned about it they became our best friends. They always said, 'Come to Hawaii,' but I never did."

At home after a shower, Ruth stands in front of the mirror. She lets the towel drop away and stares at herself. Her nipples are two dark spots on a couple of bumps. Her hips are as slim as Hank's. She could dress like a boy and pass for one. A bikini on her body will be like two ribbons tied around a stick. She thinks about Shirley, her body and how beautiful she is. Shirley's hazel eyes, glinting with speckles of blue in the sun. When Shirley said, "So many beautiful boys," Ruth felt an old sense of dread.

After class the next day at school, Ruth looks up from her desk to Miss Parker, who has come by to talk. "Ruth, I have something for you," she says. She gives Ruth a packet. Ruth shakes out a brochure and quickly reads. It is an application to a summer art program in downtown Los Angeles.

She puts it down and looks up at Miss Parker. "I only have sketches of hands."

"That's okay. Let's look and find the best ones." She pulls up a chair.

They choose four. Miss Parker helps Ruth with the application. "I'm going to mail it on my way home," Miss Parker says. A week later, a letter arrives for Ruth asking her to confirm her intention to attend and accept the scholarship they have awarded her. The first day of the program starts the day after she and Shirley are to leave for Hawaii.

Shirley stares at her, shaking her head. "It's just a stupid class!"

"It's not."

"There will be another one."

"And Hawaii will be there, it won't float away," Ruth says.

"But not *our* time."

Ruth nods. "I know."

"Look what happened when you didn't come to Mammoth. Oh, I can't believe this. Please, please, please, come?"

The art studio is near Griffith Park, in an old upstairs office building above a small grocery store. The stairway is narrow, with worn steps. The instructor is a woman who, from her last name on the brochure, Ruth expected to be Japanese, but she is Caucasian. The woman smiles and they shake hands.

"Ruth Tanazaki," Ruth says.

"Ta-na-za-ki," the woman says, sounding out each syllable with a thoughtful face, the way Kazu does when meeting someone whose family he might have known.

"I love your drawings of hands. The shapes are expressive. Drawing hands can be difficult."

The room has an air-conditioning box in the window, but it only works sometimes and never effectively. It is hot and stuffy, the bus rides there and back are long and tedious, but Ruth knows she made the right choice. It's a small group, all older than her, and they work intently for four hours each day, seldom speaking to one another. She learns about drawing and the use of watercolors. Ruth is more excited than she has ever been.

Near the end of the three-week art class Hank surprises Ruth with a visit to her room. He knocks. It is the first time he has bothered to knock that she can remember.

"What are you doing?" he asks.

"Going to check mail. Want to come?"

They walk up to Centinela Avenue where the mailbox is. They haven't done this together for a long time. Hank walks by her side, silently. A postcard has come in the mail, a photo of a large bay with turquoise water and Diamond Head in the background. She shows it to Hank.

"Why didn't you go? I would've."

They walk idly back on the dirt road. It is late afternoon, the sun is in their eyes.

"Another time. Is Tak gone?"

"Yeah."

"I heard the Kings invited you to a game?"

"That was before the garden thing."

"So?"

"So now, since everybody at school knows, they don't want to be friends with a criminal."

"You're not a criminal!"

"Maybe I am. I liked what I did."

Ruth pats him on the back and rubs his shoulder.

"I want to show you something," she says when they reach the house. In her room, Ruth takes a large portfolio from the closet. They sit together on her bed.

"I'm learning a lot in art class."

"Let me see."

She opens the portfolio.

"These are my first drawings. Compare them to the ones now."

"So much better!"

"Hands can be difficult to draw. Did you know that?"

"Are these yours, too?"

"I draw everything. Birds, trees. Here's a portrait of my art teacher. And here's a close-up of an eye."

"I could never do that."

"How do you know? Have you tried?"

"No."

"Do you want to?"

Ruth finds another sketch pad and several pencils.

"I'll show you what I learned. Nature has basic shapes. See how simple they are? Let's go outside."

They are gone for over an hour. When they return to her room, Ruth says, "You can keep the sketchpad."

"I can?"

"Yes, it's yours. These pencils, too."

"Thanks!" Hank grins, examining what she gave him. "What more can I draw?"

Ruth thinks for a moment. "Go in the backyard and draw what's left of the shed."

"It's burnt down."

"But parts are still there. The shapes are expressive. All burnt and black, like an old shipwreck."

"That's a good idea. I will!" he says. He gathers up his materials and goes outside.

She can see how pleased he is.

When Hank is gone she sits on the bed and looks through her work. She has several sketchpads by now. One is filled with early drawings of her hands. She sees the flaws, there are many, but also small improvements. Her drawings include many images. The willow tree in their front yard, their house, the table with family portraits, the closed door of her mother's room. Miss Parker's face. Her own face. She'll ask Hank and Kazu if she can draw them. And Shirley, when she returns from Hawaii. She must get her eyes exactly right.

She has begun sketching from memory. Here is a pencil drawing of the mother cat and kittens, here is the dead mud hen hanging limply from a hand by its scaly feet. And a drawing of Alice resting on the front lawn, a blanket spread beneath her. Ruth has an idea for a project, a collage of images that viewed together will create an effect. She doesn't yet know what the effect will be.

She turns the pages, looking closely at her drawings. She finds moments when she has captured what was there in life instead of what she thought was there. Sometimes the difference is just a few lines. But that difference is everything. So far, not many are as she wants them to be. Still, as she examines her drawings, she feels what she hasn't felt for a long time. Happiness, welling up inside.

Epilogue

TWENTY YEARS later, in 1985, Hank telephones Kazu as he always does on Father's Day. It is a ritual Hank dreads, never knowing what to say. He hates the small talk of these occasional calls, but after not seeing each other for so long they have little in common. Hank lives in Seattle now and Kazu in Los Angeles. His father remains as withdrawn as always. Anything that is not small talk is met by Kazu with silence at the other end of the line. Simply getting a call on this day is what Kazu seems to value most. And Hank understands. The fulfillment of the ritual is the most important part for him as well.

The telephone rings and rings but Kazu does not pick up. There is no point in leaving a message his father won't respond to. Hank calls several times throughout the day. Each time there is the long ringing of the unanswered phone. Hank tries again the next day, and the day after. On the third day after no success Hank calls the VA hospital in Westwood. "Yes, Kazu Tanazaki is a patient," the nurse says. She puts Hank on with a doctor whose voice sounds both grave and hurried. "Are you out of town? You should make arrangements. Consider coming as soon as possible."

"Yes. Thank you." Hank hangs up the phone and takes a deep breath. "I need to go to L.A.," he tells Hannah, his wife.

At the workshop he teaches, "Destruction as a Perspective to Art and Design," a freshman course in the Art Department at the

University of Washington, there are several TA's who would kill to teach the class for a week. He books a flight to LAX. At the airport he rents a car and drives straight to the hospital.

At the front desk Hank is given directions to find Kazu's room. He takes the elevator up three floors and walks along a fluorescent lit hallway, looking for the door number. He finds it and steps inside. Two elderly men, each with their own TV in a corner near the ceiling, look up. One points his remote at him. The room is not large. Flatulence and Lysol fill the air. A nurse pulls the curtain back that separates the beds.

It has been years since Hank last saw his father, and now he beholds a frail old man, unshaven, sunken cheeks, unconscious, his mouth agape. Oxygen tubes rest beneath his nose. White tape holds a cracked lens of his glasses together. He came to see his father, not this sickly person. Hank bends over to take Kazu's hand, places his forehead on it, and weeps. The two other patients watch in silence.

The doctor checks Kazu's pulse and breathing. "It won't be long," he says. A nurse carries a folding chair in for Hank and tells him where the food and beverage machines are in the hallway. In the evening another nurse brings him a blanket. In the morning, Hank awakes to see Kazu's mouth open and his chest still.

The manager of the condo where Kazu has lived for the past fifteen years gives Hank a key.

"Your father was a good man. Quiet, didn't talk much. But a good man." The manager has grayish brown hair, sun wrinkled skin and bright green eyes that seem twenty years younger than his face. He wears a red Aloha shirt with drawings of Diamond Head.

"Thank you," says Hank. They shake hands.

He cleans his father's condo, taking old food and trash downstairs to a dumpster in the alley behind the building. He puts canned food in a box for the food bank. He drives around the neighborhood to see what has changed. The dirt road and old house are still there.

He parks and gets out of the car to stare at the house, imagining the rooms inside and remembering being in them. He looks through the fence at the creek. The tide is low, there are islands of sand and pools of water. The fields next to the house have been replaced by housing units. The willow tree is gone. Now a chain link fence runs through where it used to be. He wishes he could find the person who cut it down.

There is no one to visit in Los Angeles. Tak never returned from Japan. He became a priest at a temple in Kyoto. Hank still receives letters. Tak says his favorite activity as a priest is hitting people with a stick when he sees their minds are wandering. *Come to Japan*, Tak writes. But Hank doesn't believe he will ever go.

Shirley Carson moved to the Big Island, where she married and had children. Although he didn't know her well, they exchanged letters every now and then, her letters always ending with, *Come stay with us and meet my family.* But he never went, and after a time they stopped writing.

For years, Hank kept in touch with Mr. Nice, inviting him to Seattle. Then one day he received a letter from a family member saying that Mr. Nice had passed away.

There are unopened bottles of whisky in the condo. His father was not much of a solo drinker. Gifts, Hank guesses. He looks carefully at the bottoms for marks people make to see if years later the gift they gave comes back. He doesn't find any marks, but it's hard to tell. Some marks are cleverly disguised as a smudge from the shelf, a nick on the label. Kazu kept an actual record of the marks he made, chuckling to himself when he received a gift that years before he had given away. Marks or no marks, Hank opens a bottle and pours himself a drink, then begins to sort through Kazu's personal things. He finds nothing surprising. Enema bags, seals, ointments, and other paraphernalia Kazu used for his colostomy. A cigar box with the purple heart and silver star. A box of men's magazines beneath the bed that Hank flips through. There is a box of what looks like his mother's things. Old make-up, cheap jewelry, some clothes, a bundle of letters, her Bible. Hank will seal it up and ship it to Seattle and decide what to do with it then.

He puts Kazu's underwear into a trash bag for the dumpster, his pants and shirts and the single suit into another bag to drop off at the homeless shelter the next day.

A cardboard tube leans in the corner of the closet. He looks inside, then pours another drink to examine the contents further. This he puts away by his suitcase along with Kazu's war medals.

The days until the funeral are spent cleaning, trips up and down the stairs to the dumpster, hiring people to come and take the bigger items away.

The service is held at the same church as for Alice. It's a different pastor, though, a Japanese American man Hank's age who knew Kazu and speaks of his patriotism and bravery. The audience is much smaller than for Alice. An even smaller group follows the hearse to the cemetery for burial. Mostly older men. Hank recognizes some of them. Melon Watanabe, Hash Hashimoto, and even Eto. They come to say hello. For a moment Hank imagines they are the Three Kings, now aged and decrepit. They shake his hand, look him up and down, and say, in their reedy voices, "All grown up now." They tell Hank that Kazu had been proud of him.

"Dr. Kiyonaga?" Hank asks.

"Died last year. Pancreatic cancer."

There is no gathering planned. The crowd disperses. Hank intends to stay after everyone leaves, to see the grave filled. A respectful distance away are two men smoking, leaning against the large tires of a parked tractor.

Eto, thick and hunched over like an old bear, is among the last to leave. He comes and stands a moment with Hank near the open grave. Hank knows the man has never liked him.

"All three together now," Eto said.

"Yes."

Eto stares at him. "Married and with a son. You turned out good. But, an artist."

"A daughter. And yes, I am."

"You make money?"

"I teach."

"Ah," Eto says. "Well, goodbye."

Hank remains, the last one, then realizes the men with the tractor are waiting for him to leave. He drives to another part of the cemetery, parks under a shade tree and steps out of the car to smoke and check his watch. When he returns, Kazu's grave is filled and a green tarp covers the dirt.

The headstone for Kazu will be installed in a few days. He will be back in Seattle by then and won't see it. Hank squats down and pulls weeds and cleans the headstones of Alice and Ruth.

Towards the end of the summer when Ruth's art program ended, Hank remembers sensing a change in her. She stopped asking him so many dumb questions, she seemed happy, joking around and making sarcastic remarks about people they knew. She was funny like she used to be.

One night, during dinner, Kazu said that more girls than ever were attending college, and that meant competition for husbands on campus would be at an all-time high. He said, "Competition," nodding his head like he was talking about a sports game. Ruth interrupted him. "I'm not going to college to meet a husband," she said.

Kazu looked at her in shock.

"If I go to college at all, it will be to art school."

There was silence. Hank kept his head down, eating quietly, glancing at their father's face. It looked bewildered and perhaps a little frightened. Hank couldn't believe Ruth said what she did.

No one spoke for the rest of dinner.

As Ruth and Hank cleaned the kitchen, the loud sounds of a ballgame came from the bathroom where enema night was in progress. It was a time they could talk freely in the kitchen without fear of being overheard.

They were at the sink, Ruth washing dishes and handing them to Hank for drying. He was surprised again by Ruth's next announcement.

She looked at him, smiling the way she used to when suggesting something mischievous.

"Guess what? Tomorrow I'm going sailing."

"With who?"

"A boy, John."

"Does dad know?"

"No. But it's okay. It's just a little boat, and John's a good sailor. We'll stay in the harbor."

The way she said it, like it was something she did every day.

Hank swept the floor, wishing he could go sailing, too.

It was in the early evening of the next day when Hank learned that John took them far past the entrance of the harbor and into the open sea. A windstorm had risen suddenly and John, who had sailed only once before, capsized the small boat. He saved himself by clinging to the overturned hull.

Hank cleans Ruth's bronze gravestone, rubbing in small circles with the soapy washcloth.

At Ruth's funeral John had appeared from among the trees, a thin specter dressed in a worn black suit, bearing a limp handful of flowers to Hank and Kazu. He continually brushed away longish dark hair from blue eyes that were wide open and unblinking. Small sobs escaped him. He wanted to explain what happened that day. "I owe it to you both," he said. Hank glanced at his father and saw that Kazu was breathing slowly, calming himself. But when John pointed out why it had been impossible, even foolish, for him to try and save Ruth, though she was only ten feet from where he clung to the hull, Kazu drew back and stared at the boy. Whatever John saw in that look made him drop his eyes and fall silent.

Finished cleaning, Hank stares at the dates on Ruth's headstone. She was only sixteen years old.

He sits for a while on the grass. The cemetery is on a hillside and he can see the harbor of San Pedro below. A small tree shades him in the hot afternoon.

It wasn't until long after Ruth was gone that Hank understood what she meant to him. She wanted what he wanted, and it took years for him to understand what that was. It was freedom. Freedom to become what he would become if left to his own. He couldn't name it then, but looking back he can see. Their sad family and the caring, stern community. What a narrow road they had to walk. He tried, but he didn't know how. Ruth could have done it, easily. She was brave. Braver than him, braver than anyone. But she chose a different way and showed him what it was. He pulls at the grass. Grandparents die, parents die, children die. Death in that order is good. But Ruth had been too soon. It happened many years ago, yet grief visits him unexpectedly. Rising up, receding back into a mysterious place. Love and regret rushing through him in waves out of nowhere.

The plane touches down in Seattle and his wife and daughter are there to meet him. Little Ruth, three years old, already knows how to ask what present he brought her from Los Angeles.

"A nice t-shirt. It says Santa Monica Beach."

At home he unpacks and goes to his study. He opens the cardboard tube and spreads several drawings on a work desk, examining them closely.

"Hannah, you and Ruthie come look."

He unrolls the largest drawing and puts weights on the edges to hold it flat.

"It's Ruth's work."

The little girl Ruth stands on her tiptoes to see.

"The hands are wonderful," Hannah says, leaning over to study it, tucking a strand of long blond hair behind her ear. "And the landscape. Hank, she was so talented."

The pencil drawing is of trees, a bird bath, and a few stone pillars lying randomly on the ground as if whatever they were meant for had been abandoned. A million tree leaves seem to undulate in shades of black and gray.

"The pillars are odd," Hannah says.

Hank studies the drawings. They are immature. She was young, still in high school, but her talent was real. If only her talent had been given more time to grow.

He unrolls another large drawing, a collage of small sketches. There are faces: him, Kazu, Alice. There are faces of Shirley Carson, one of a dark-haired boy he thinks must be John, and others he does not know. Ruth's self-portraits appear several times. There are drawings of parts of their old house, the arched hallway near Alice's bedroom, a closed door, the small living room table with family photos, the kitchen table with four plates. He sees the willow that used to be in their front yard, the eucalyptus trees, flower gardens, pools of water, birds, snakes, and the fields. There are images he recognizes from their childhood and others known only to her. Small hands are placed throughout, they tug at and shape the drawing. It appears haphazard and random. The piece is unfinished, with sections jammed and crowded with images, and others empty. He gently touches the thick paper. His wife and daughter have left the room, and he is glad, not only because his eyes are teary. He sniffles, blinks, wipes his eyes, and makes sure the door is locked. Hank opens the window and puts a small fan there facing outside. He needs a cigarette and the rule is that his daughter never sees him. He lights one and examines Ruth's drawing more closely, turning his head to exhale smoke in the direction of the window, holding the cigarette down at his side as he bends forward, trying to get a feel for what she had in mind.

Acknowledgements

In Memory of Raymond Hummel, 11th September 1958–12th September 2019. ~ *To a better set of problems* ~

Many thanks to…

Dan DeWeese for publishing this book. His creative instincts, integrity, and multiple areas of expertise made it a satisfying and fun project.

Elizabeth McKenzie, from the beginning, whose encouragement and kind words got me here.

Steven Okazaki, for pushing me to do better and showing me how.

Charles Johnson, for his mentorship over the years.

Bob Nakamura and Coleen Lee, for their thoughtful suggestions.

My family, who has helped me through the most challenging of times. Adah, Akira, Zahra and Grace. We will always be together.

Thanks to F.O.G., for the food, drinks, conversation, and friendship. You know who you are.

About the Author

Ben Masaoka (1952-2024), born and raised in Los Angeles, was a trianglist for many years between Los Angeles, Seattle, and Hawaii. He traded the sun for the tall, dark green trees of the Northwest, and his short stories were published in the *Chicago Review of Books* and *Catamaran Literary Reader*. He is survived by his wife, three children, and a dog. He had a good life. Was happy to be here.